JOHN
⇒⋯AND⋯⇐
ANZIA
⇒⋯AN⋯⇐
AMERICAN
ROMANCE

OTHER BOOKS BY NORMA ROSEN

Joy to Levine!
Green
Touching Evil
At the Center

NORMA ROSEN

JOHN AND ANZIA

AN AMERICAN ROMANCE

E. P. DUTTON · NEW YORK

Published in the United States by E. P. Dutton,
a division of Penguin Books USA Inc.,
2 Park Avenue, New York, N.Y. 10016.

Published simultaneously in Canada by
Fitzhenry and Whiteside, Limited, Toronto.

Library of Congress Cataloging-in-Publication Data

Rosen, Norma.
John and Anzia : an American romance / Norma Rosen. — 1st ed.
p. cm.
ISBN 0-525-24806-4
1. Dewey, John, 1859–1952—Fiction. 2. Yezierska, Anzia,
1880?–1970—Fiction. I. Title.
PS3568.O77J64   1989   89-1497
813'.54—dc20   CIP

Designed by Rocco Piscatello, Jr.

1 3 5 7 9 10 8 6 4 2

First Edition

To the memory of my father
Louis Gangel
who knew the Lower East Side as closely as Anzia
and who struggled as fiercely to be free of it
and to my husband
Robert Samuel Rosen
latecomer to America
who teaches me new ways to see it

Miniatures

And fervent heat dissolve away
The loins of fire and head of grey.
> —from untitled poem
> by JOHN DEWEY

"He had left the track of generations of puritan training and burst into this blaze of life. And she . . . had longed for the . . . intimacy of that other race that had always been locked to her."
> —*All I Could Never Be*,
> by ANZIA YEZIERSKA

"It is obvious from the nature of the perceptive process that a defect in any of its aspects results in faulty perception, and, perforce, stunted experience."
> —"Learning to See," *The Art of Renoir*,
> by ALBERT C. BARNES

"Of course you can tell it is a finished picture . . . you can tell because it has a frame, now whoever heard of anybody framing a canvas if the picture isn't finished."
> —*The Autobiography of Alice B. Toklas*,
> by GERTRUDE STEIN

Foreword

They could hardly have been more polar: John Dewey (1859–1952), a world-famous philosopher of New England stock; Anzia Yezierska (1880?–1970), an impoverished Jewish immigrant from Poland. We know almost nothing about their love affair except that it was brief—it began in 1917 and ended within a year—and affected each of them profoundly.

Dewey's impassioned love poems were discovered after both were dead. Without that unearthing, it is not likely that the affair would have come to light at all. In the late 1970s, a university press edition of Dewey's poems revealed a piece of scholarly detective work on typewriter-key faces and paper watermarks that sleuthed out the connection to Yezierska, whose stories were found to contain lines echoed—as if deep forces had hurled them there—in Dewey's poems.

The poems had been thrown away, salvaged, secreted in the Columbia University archives, forgotten, and rediscovered. Dewey covered his tracks as well as he could. Colleagues may have suspected, but they remained silent. Yezierska altered facts to suit her stories and the restrictions of the time—an era of melting-pot heat, rage for Americanization, and grudge-filled boundaries. We know better now but live with the legacy—old stock/immigrant, aristocrat/ethnic, and dozens more of these dualities whose breach we say we long to heal.

What drew them together? What drove them apart? And what took place in between? These are questions only fiction can answer now.

A further question—why not leave them in peace; why uncover what they, especially Dewey, tried so hard to suppress?—is answered for me in the poems themselves. Having worked their way up from burial, they seem to be addressing us. We are bidden to take notice. Once upon a time, there really was a John and an Anzia. Then what happened?

"In imagination as in fact we know a road only by what we see as we travel on it," John Dewey wrote.

This book grew from traveling imagination's road. There are facts here, too. In an afterword I will attempt to separate them from the fictions—theirs and mine.

NEW YORK

1

Wings More Plucked than Feathered

ANZIA

It's not yet dawn. I feel the mended place in my shirtwaist where it molds over my breast. My heart bangs away beneath my fingers, a clamor I have stopped attending to. It's just as well to dress in the dark and not see boots that blacking can't cover the scuff on, a hat that flies a pair of wings more plucked than feathered.

"Can't you be an eagle and carry me where I need to go?" I'm talking to that dead bird on the hat, there's no one else. Why not quibble with a hat brim if the room and your mood are both dark? "Never mind, this time I'll carry you."

By now a quarrel of voices and the thump and screek of pushcart wheels are flying into my window from Rivington Street. A mixture of smells, food and garbage, floats on the sound. The pretzel vendor whistles shrilly on the corner, and I inhale the heavy gravelings of salt. In the darkness the loaf of bread on the table looks made of wood. I've already lifted a piece to my lips and put it back. If you can't swallow you shouldn't eat.

Uptown, where I'm going, women donate ankles to the war effort. They mince around in hobble hems. My broad skirt sweeps

3

the uneven floor, heavy serge that lasts. You have to move fast or it weighs you down. I like to move quickly anyway and can drive a broom around my four walls in one minute flat, a room so small it sticks in a seam of the ghetto like a piece of lint. Before I can leave it, someone knocks. My sister pokes her head around the door, then her bosom with a boa draped over it— even on a September day, even in the heat. The sight of her traps my tongue. News from home is never good.

"What's wrong?" I manage a whisper.

"Just I can't be home to fix Papa's food. Oh, do it for me, Anzia." She begins to dance around on her toes. "Oh, please!" For a second I'm startled. From where does this idea come to a woman of how to get something in this life—hop up and down, laugh and beg, or, if not, cry?

Before I hear, I guess at what she wants: to spend the day with a man who plans outings on time off from work or from no work at all, except what it costs him to charm out her wages. Her wide eyes shift around, her body can't keep still, her lips break into smiles that in one minute might slide toward sobs.

I have to remind her, "Papa won't want to see me."

"Oh, please, he will! Papa likes you, you're the smart one!"

"I have to be someplace," I say. The wide eyes fill with tears. "All right. Don't be unhappy. I'll go."

After I kiss her, she begins a little pirouette, her pretty face flushed with joy.

"Don't be too happy, either. Think what you're doing." Be careful, be wiser, I mean. Not like me.

She loops the feathery snake around my neck and says, "*You* be happy."

I have to shift away from that and how it's meant. I ask what man is better than night school—and my sister shrieks with nervous laughter. As for me, the word "school" makes me sweat—the one I'm going to and the one I'm not going to. What will the Settlement House ladies say? Mrs. Morgenstern and Mrs. Warburg and Mrs. Kahn and Mrs. Mendelsohn, Mrs. Wealthy and Mrs. Scrub-Your-Hands and Mrs. Dress-Nice and Mrs. Remember-the-Others-Are-Watching-You—what will they say when they hear I haven't turned up to teach their cooking class today?

The steamy streets already swarm with pushcarts, hawkers, trundlers of every kind of merchandise. In all the muck and pile-up, there is always the possibility of a mouse nibbling at some corner, to make a tiny hole and let in a little air. I will be a mouse that never sleeps. . . .

Hurrying up the stairs to Papa's room, I nearly trip on a crumbling tread. Talmud is an ocean. Why do only eels and scorpions get fished out for me?

His room is bare except for a cot and books piled before him on his table at the window. Pages quiver under his fingers like live creatures swimming from the foam of his white beard.

"Papa, it's Anzia."

He makes no sign that he knows any Anzia. For good measure, he shields his eyes with one hand. In the meantime this Anzia he doesn't know searches in the kitchen for a plate for his bread and herring, a silvered spoon for his glass so the boiling tea won't crack it. When the Anzia he doesn't know backs through the door with the glass and the dish, he bends lower and confides to his books, "What is she? A woman alone. Not a wife, not a mother."

The glass in my hand begins to click against the saucer. Be grateful, I tell myself. He sees at least that you exist.

"She has no existence," my father says.

Both of us are trembling. The small tufts of white beard under his lip count some woman's sins. No one chases her, yet she runs. No Cossack or Tsar. Not pursued, wanting to pursue. She is cursed, lost, her way dark, her life . . . her life. . . .

My life. . . .

I am terrified that he will burst into sobs. He turns it into a fit of coughing instead, and I hurry forward with his tea.

"Be careful, Papa. Blow. It's hot."

He takes a scalding sip. He blows a sigh into his pages.

"*Here* matters." He caresses the riffled book leaves. "This."

I breathe out words almost without sound. "Whatever I learned of reading and writing came from watching, Papa. You."

He blows his nose and stares into his pages. He sighs heavily again, because the Anzia he doesn't know so resembles yet resists him.

In the street I see how much time I've lost! But nervous energy is boiling up in me so that I have to walk. Manhattan is split in two. War is the poultice applied to the break. On every block, from Lower East Side slums to neighborhoods of wealth, the song unrolls like bandage: "Over there!" Young men in uniform stare at me. "Hello, Miss Blue Eyes." "Hello, Redhead!" "What do you put on that complexion, peaches and cream?" I stare too. Khaki shirts and knickers. Better to dress like them. What good are clothes like mine when I'm bound for battle? An old man in a poster gives me an angry look and points his finger. UNCLE SAM WANTS YOU! Nobody can have me till I get what I need. . . .

"Selfish! A woman who does that is selfish!" Whose voice is that? Papa's. One of my sisters. I can't remember and begin to think it might be my own. . . . I hate starting to cry while I walk, but better than on the trolley, people staring, relieved to see someone else has it worse. The air dries your tears, the wind blows them away.

The soldiers have wrappings on their shins, as if already wounded. Poor young men! They watch me go, they drink in every woman's colors. Girls are their flag. For a few blocks, I worry about the ones I see along the way: a boy with red hair like mine, another who is tall and gawky with a lick of brown hair over one eye, and a healthy open-faced one, laughing at a joke. Then dearer faces swim up in my head, and keener worries, only waiting for the chance to get at me: my child . . . my family . . . my child. . . . I stride faster, I feel my color heighten, and the soldiers call, "Hey, Blue Eyes!" "Hey, Redhead!" "Hey, Peaches and Cream!"

At Twenty-third Street, where Fifth and Broadway cross, a crowd is gathered at the Flatiron Building, spilling into the broad avenues like the sea beneath a ship's prow. Office workers lean from windows like passengers at portholes, waving flags and flinging out paper streamers. At the crowd's edge someone screams, "It's Pickford and Fairbanks! It's War Bonds!"

"Oh, let me see!" a woman cries. I step aside so she can twist her neck for a view of a platform where yellow curls are bouncing and a pair of red pantaloons leaps into the air.

The woman claps applause like prayers to heaven. Then, in the disappointment of nothing more to see, she crosses her gloved hands on the silver knob of her umbrella and turns to where I'm catching my breath, looking at the ground. From her immense, flower-covered hat floats the splendor of respectability.

"Not very patriotic, are you. Don't know who that was, do you. You people should learn the culture of your new country."

I am memorizing the gloves, the umbrella, the hat. How will they go into words?

The plumes on the woman's head wave around as if they smell something bad. In a low voice, but not that low, she asks her companion, "What are they letting into the country now?"

The same as they let in when you came, I'd like to say, but words wilt in my mouth. I see by the building's big clock how time is flying and I fly myself, from beneath the hanging banners.

Remembrance comes flying along too.

The Sunday before, Levitas had refused me a sight of my child. *"Now* you want to see her? When before this you saw fit to leave?"

"Only for a little while, I told you." The sound of my voice like the squeak of a mouse.

"And this." Waving a letter in my face. "Why not ask for the moon!" Standing before the apartment door, the scuffed wooden panels at his back, reading my words with a mimicking sound: " 'If only I had money for a better place to live and could keep her with me.' 'This is some Anzia!' my mother said when I told her!"

This-is-some-Anzia had already seen from his face what would be his answer to her note. Was it such a terrible thing to ask?

He shouted so the whole building could hear. "Not only our child! Your own people also! In Poland, Russia—pogroms! You want to learn? Now?" A few neighbors' doors creaked. "When the whole world shakes? When the Jews of Kishinev scream in our ears?"

How? This-is-some-Anzia asked herself. How did I come to have two fathers?

He loosened his collar and began another way. Hot kisses spilled over my face, my neck, my breasts. I pushed back with my hands; he pushed forward with his hips. Through his respectable dark trousers and the heavy serge of my skirt, I felt his fever heat. Poor man, not even drafted to the army but wounded anyway.

"No," I pleaded. "Didn't we agree it would be no?"

"A man like me, am I equipped to agree with such a thing?"

7

Nothing in his life had prepared him for this injustice. A decent, hard-working man. An immigrant. Who married another. Books had made my dreams spin away from his. If I tried to write a story with such a woman in it, any reader would despise her.

After that I sat on a bench in Central Park and imagined I felt my child's arms tight about my neck, the weight of Louise's light body in my lap. *Only for a little while.* We would play the game of writers. No charge for that. "Describe what you see, Mama." "A fat man eating ice cream like a polar bear lapping." Her collar blew back against our faces like a hanky blotting tears. But we were too quick, too gay, too imaginative for tears. Busy and chattering every minute, with a hug and a kiss every other. At the end she would go cheerfully indoors to her father with some new project, leaves from the park to trace or pebbles to paint. See, it can be done, it's all possible, not just dreams!

Except that the touch on my neck was only the breeze, and the weight in my lap was a book whose print blurred when I looked. Everything has come full circle and you are trapped inside, I told myself. When you couldn't read English there was hope, you could learn. Now you can't read because you're crying. What will you hope for next? When I wiped my eyes I thought, I'll tell Levitas I'm coming back, and then I'll see her. This way is too hard. . . .

A squirrel dropped a nut at my feet and looked up as if to say, "You can't have mine. Find your own." "New republic," one man said to another at the end of the bench. "By God, the new republic." America, I translated, eavesdropping before I knew it. They were discussing America's role in the war.

"Do we," he said. "That's right." The other nodded. "Do we, by God. And that spells it out." Do we? Not we do? When I finally understood, No, they meant a magazine and a man, my heart, which had already sunk to the bottom, seemed to fail me altogether at the thought of so much left to learn before I could claim my place. There in the park they named a book that mingled with the music seeping from the street: *Democracy*—"Send the word, send the word"—*and Education.*

Later at the Education Alliance I turned its pages. The masses required their special path to education, said Dewey. Do we . . . ?

At 116th Street and Broadway I feel lightheaded and wobbly. I press into one cheek and breast an iron bar of the gate that guards Columbia University. Beyond it I glimpse columns and domes, flights of marble stairs, carved statues and land-scaped gardens set like jewels around an open plaza. My heart—again my heart! it runs and bounces and sinks and rises like a boat on a stormy sea. Now I feel how it tears from my chest—like what? Like a dog, like a racehound that leaps the fence and runs to sniff among those beauties. If not me, then my child will come here. I soothe my heart with the thought, like a trembling beast I try to calm.

What woman does what you think of doing? That voice I know—my mother's, shocked and frightened. When I was little I played the game of choosing with my sisters. Would you rather be Rachel or Leah? A joke! If you wanted to be Miriam or Deborah they looked at you. *Again* you're marching over everybody? Be Rebekah. Let fate find you. Only be beautiful and mind your business, draw good luck like water from a well. There was nothing wrong with being Rachel, either. Not exactly lazy—she stole her father's idols. Rebekah schemed to make an heir of the child *she* chose, not her husband . . . a busy life!

I think about a story I may write. An immigrant woman struggling to make a home for her family. A loud, swift quarrel with the loutish landlord. It's not Tolstoy, though I study his books and vow to keep in mind, at the moment of writing, the calm sentences, the slow unfolding, the trust in each stroke. Nothing stops my own gallop. I snatch what I can into words. Exclamation points hold my sentences together like corset stays. You never trust that anyone will want to hear what you know. You never trust yourself. I am thinking it like two exclamation points.

The last four blocks uptown, to the red-brick building of Teachers College, are the worst of the walk. Thick stones clump around the windows, so that looking out or in gets weighted down. The registrar, with black ribbons dangling from his pinch-nose spectacles, is like an undertaker come to bury me. He calls me "Miss" in a curt, scolding tone.

"A certificate to teach at the settlement house, Miss, is something you ought to feel grateful for, not complaining. You certainly don't qualify for more!"

I'm amazed he can't see a difference. With only a certificate to teach Domestic Science, what can I learn? What can I earn? My dream is concocted from reading, but what's wrong with that? Louise will come and live with me. There will be music lessons, leather schoolbags for books, a nursemaid for the times I'm conducting classes—at a high school, not a settlement house. . . .

"Real subjects!" I cry. "Literature, history . . . !"

The undertaker-registrar shakes his black ribbons. Too late, I wake to the fact that this is no way to approach him. Couldn't you remember, no outburst this time? He is thrusting an ink-stained palm before my eyes. He slams the coffin lid of his office door in my face.

A clerk in arm garters, seeing me stripped of hope, teeters back in his chair as I pass. He doesn't mind pinching my bottom even if I am a corpse. I feel the fumbling touch but don't stop to swing my string bag. I am already moving. I run, my black wool shawl trailing. I am like my sister with her boa. I wear or carry this shawl all the time. It was my mother's: a slum shawl. I fling it sometimes over one shoulder and tuck it into my belt, Spanish style. To hold onto it as part of my dress, yet vary its use somehow—I need to do that. I tell myself I want to bring my mother's lost life somehow forward into mine. How can that be—comfort my mother, who is dead, rather than be comforted myself with her shawl? It sounds foolish even to my own ears, arrogant. But if your mother, living, hadn't known how to reach you because your dreams were too foreign and frightening, then you must somehow fling over a bridge to reach her—however queerly, however late. Will that be how my Louise one day feels? Will she trail some kind of shawl and dream it is a bridge to me?

The thought makes me run faster. The place I'm going to now will build a realer bridge than dreaming to the life we both need. Not until the cobbles slide beneath my boots do I notice pouring rain. Downtown. Four blocks. Inside Columbia's gates, Alma Mater sits on her throne. One hand holds up a torch; the other extends in a gesture that might be welcome or reproof. I cross the quadrangle, climb the marble steps, and touch the cold lap. I stare at the indifferent face carved from the snows of clear-eyed thought. The wreathed brow, hung with drops, is level with my own.

"I'm here," I whisper into the statue's ear.

Then I plant myself in the path of a hurrying student, who calls out directions before he slips by me. I pick a building, praying I am right, and have a choice of running up one flight of stairs or down another. I pick the up, of course, and run. I'd sooner go home than down. Inside, the air is cooler and bears traces of a recent ammonia washing. The smell rushes up my nose with a familiar sting. But in a corridor, as I bend to tie a loosened bootlace, doubt comes over me like darkness. I am shabby, ignorant. My fingers shake. My breath blows so hot it dries in my throat. Dizzy, I walk toward a fountain of marble and bronze, carved with dark cherubs.

I want to be in my room. I want to be there writing down my dreams, instead of so foolishly trying to make them happen. What *can* happen except that my heart will bang itself to pieces inside my chest? I want to write it: "She is not a tall woman. In those high-ceilinged halls she shrinks." Don't ever say in English, I remind myself, weary of all my mistakes, that a person's shortness is heightened by the highness of the ceiling. How can shortness be heightened?

After that I stoop to suck a jet of water into my parched mouth. I rehearse some words, but get no further than: "Professor Dewey. . . ." What is it I want to say? Even my thoughts stutter: "Professor Dewey . . . Professor, excuse me, Professor. . . ." Trembling, losing my breath, my mouth dry again, I push open a door. A man is stooping, as I stooped over the water seconds before. Crumpled sheets of yellow paper writhe around him on the floor as he tries to gather them together.

He says an amazing thing. "The old manure balls got away from me again, Bill." Then he looks up and sees I'm not Bill. I see that not all scholars are old and white-bearded like my father.

The room wobbles dizzyingly. "Professor Dewey—"

He is a slow-moving man, but he springs up nimbly as I sink toward the floor.

He catches me in his arms.

2 ...≼

Can I Learn That?

Springing and sinking and catching—yes, fine. But a few where/ when/hows wouldn't hurt. Take it from someone (a voice from the woodwork, a talking horse) who spent too many early years in confusion. Because Anzia dived in feet- or heart-first, breathless, hasty, reckless, frantic to pound in her point as if fearful of death or deportation, must her story do the same? Especially if we're talking here about how everything turns to its opposite?

Slowly, then. Plod. How could it all come about, This-is-some-Anzia's morning dash to Columbia and Dewey's (not-at-all-dewy: dry! dry!) embrace? Who was she; who was he? Anzia heard of John Dewey on a park bench. Later she learned about the volumes he published on education, filled with ideas called "progressive" by the world, but never by him. If he'd called those ideas anything it would have been "self-evident" or "plain common sense." He argued that minds should not be stuffed with facts in disregard of their own development. Students should learn by doing, consulting their own experience (even six-year-olds have experience—Anzia's own child!). Questions that spring from life experience must be allowed to lead beautifully and naturally to what the self needs to learn next. ("Should I dump this bucket of mud in the yard, teacher, or on the floor?" "Why not try it and see for yourself?" Splash! Smear! "I see that I never want to dump a bucket of mud on the floor again. But I will dump it in the yard where I can pat it into a useful little fortress, dried in the sun, and my puppy can sleep inside. I am also now interested in reading about others who made creative uses of mud.") This was John Dewey's pure and respectful view of human beings and their inner wisdom. Decades after he and Anzia parted, Dewey's ideas suffered their own dialectical demise as people longed once more for the structures of old-style head-stuffing education. ("What was the first recorded use of mud to construct habitable huts?" "In 1851, the Scottish explorer David Livingstone ventured into the interior of Africa, where he discovered huts ingeniously fashioned by natives along the mud-abundant banks of the Zambezi River." "Excellent: A.") Aridity of method seemed a small price to pay compared to the confusions of a form of schooling that appeared to be all outgo from the self and little intake. Pendulums have all eternity to swing in, but human beings must catch their rides on them at their own moments. When Yezierska met Dewey, his ideas, sunk like sweet raisins at the bottom of large lumps of doughy Dewey prose, were exactly what she needed to hear.

Human life itself, Dewey wrote, is no more static than the pendulum. Each new phase of life is experienced by the being you are at that moment. But also each new experience (properly reflected upon) alters that being, so that the next phase is experienced by someone not quite the same as who you were before. Not only that. Reality is always changing too, according to who is perceiving and interacting with it. Altogether, it seems, life is something like a fun-house floor. The boards shift back, forth, and sideways, and you, the person on them, sway and tilt and shift in response, but also you make the floor shift and wobble even more with each step. (Or so it appeared to Anzia, unstable and shaken life-experiencer that she was.) Is it any wonder that an admiring nation bestowed on John Dewey an affectionate nickname? He was the "Common-Sense Philosopher." He was also a married man, father of a numerous family, and women and men alike ought to deplore the deception of his loved ones about to unfold.

And This-is-some-Anzia, who was she? Author of nothing much when we meet her. A woman who fled a stifling marriage and left her child, shockingly, to the father's care while she ventured out in search of education and self-fulfillment. She took with her a heart made fierce by aches and longings, a brain imprinted with pathetic tag ends of autodidact's learning. We certainly must deplore Anzia's actions as well.

Having deplored what is deplorable, we ought to get on with their story. It's bound to engender, one way or another, more deplorableness. Given America, given its distant reaches like some vast stage swept bare in readiness for dramatic collisions, can we wonder at their meeting, however unlikely? Can we wonder that what happened afterward, so startling and shaking (that fun-house floor!) caused them agony as well as joy? So much experience! Yet by the end it seems that only one of them allowed experience to sink in deep enough to effect change. Which one would you expect that to be, the prophet of change and growth or the immigrant ghetto girl? In matters of change and growth, the answer is always: Not what you expect!

The next day Anzia again came to Columbia's campus. Again she caught a student on the fly. This time she asked directions to Professor Dewey's class.

"I can locate the space for you," the student replied. "That's no guarantee he will occupy it."

"What is that in plain English?"

"In plain English the professor is seldom where he's supposed to be. Even if he's there he might be somewhere else."

"Where is somewhere else?" It was better to feel exasperated than frightened. "Tell me where to find him. He invited me to his class. I don't want to miss it. Please!"

This was after Anzia's heart-thudding thrust through Dewey's door. After her faint into Dewey's grasp. We can imagine that grasp, shocked and timid. But also, in the way of such things, ravenously greedy, with a knowing/unknowing and puritanically scrupulous placing of Dewey's fingers, so as not to brush (but burningly aware of them all the same!) her breasts. Anzia had aroused Dewey's sympathy. Let that stand for other arousals too. She received an invitation to attend his seminar on Social and Political Philosophy, and was nervous enough without mysteries.

The student relented. But still with mischief in his glance, which shifted over Anzia's form as freely as the load of new books shifted in his arms. "Lecture hall. Leaning on a window-sill, probably, looking into the street, scheming his escape. But of course he's thinking. His concentration is so wonderful he can lose track of where he is and who's with him—about a hundred and fifty students, I'd say, including the society ladies who dote on his ideas, all waiting with their pens in the air—"

"One hundred and fifty! I'll never find a seat," Anzia cried.

"Well—in the first days. After a few weeks you can have any seat you want. Only diehards will be left. You can't hear him, his sentences never get finished, and he doesn't know you're there in the first place because he won't look at you. Odd behavior for someone whose field is education, don't you think?"

The student was flirting with her, but Anzia hardly noticed. "My God!" she said. "Another one who likes to torture people."

"Oh, no, a kind man," the student said. "Never fails anybody. Shy. Distracted by the war. Or by his own genius thoughts. Some say"—the student smiled, flirting with Anzia a little more— "the professor is dreaming of a lady he's secretly in love with. A joke. Everyone knows he's respectably married, with a house full of children. If he ever had a secret meeting with a lady he'd forget the time and place it was set for, and probably her name as well."

The student turned regretfully away from his teasing. "I have my own class to get to. Up those steps, turn right, and good luck."

The hard marbleized cover of Anzia's new notebook banged against her chest. The fresh-sharpened pencils she held in her fist clacked against one another. What are you shaking for, idiot? She moved among the milling students with their new clothes, their shiny leather briefcases, no different from other flesh and blood. But they seemed, joking and jostling, hearts light, another race. For them there was neither poverty nor war.

From the doorway, Anzia looked into an immense lecture room with rising rows of seats. She saw that the graduate students took their places at the front. The society ladies, carrying the professor's volumes in gloved hands, moved to the back. A golden light from tall windows fell upon them all.

"I don't belong at the front, and not at the back either." Anzia in her fright said it to the graduate student coming with her through the door. She was comforting herself with the sound of a voice, even if it was her own. "I'm between Scylla and Charybdis," she said, to show: not exactly ignorant! Scylla and Charybdis, a phrase from her full-of-gaps reading, were for all she knew two avenues in Minsk.

"Really?" The graduate student stared, faintly smiled, and then hurried to a seat.

Front or back you won't fool anybody, so sit, Anzia told herself. She slid into the seat nearest her at the front.

On the platform Professor Dewey looked taller, thinner. Behind his round glasses he gazed out with the full stare, curious and shy at the same time, of a young man, though his hair was beginning to whiten. It was center-parted, straight and fine, not packed into pleats like hers, ghetto hair waiting to spring out. A silky panel of it fell across a forehead that was as broad and clear as Alma Mater's in the courtyard. A full bottom lip was almost concealed by a rich mustache, thick and brown. He resembled—now it came to her—the writer Robert Louis Stevenson, whose picture she had seen in the frontispiece of a book of poems. Stevenson's good looks were calm. Under Dewey's quietness, Anzia saw, a dark river ran. She also saw that this face before her had no idea of its handsomeness. And probably of no one else's, either. Didn't he—doesn't a philosopher—see only what was behind his brow?

When the lecture began, his voice was low. Around the edges, a light, pleasant hoarseness. From the country, Anzia decided. From the open air. In that voice, after he'd caught her in his arms and held on to her till she recovered, then slowly set her on her feet, he had invited her to join his seminar. Both stood by then with pinkened cheeks, as if her faint, his astonished catch, the surprise every part of her body was feeling, were all as good as a walk in the wind.

Looking up at him on the platform, she saw that one of his socks was blue, the other brown. A piece of material flapped at his side where his jacket pocket ought to have been. Did he wander among his thoughts with lighted eyes? Blind and blundering among objects of this world, though, tearing bits of himself on edges of desks and doorknobs.

Once in a while he remembered that his voice might not be heard at the back of the room (she thanked God she sat at the front) and raised it on whatever was about to pass his lips—"come" or "go" or "maybe"—before his voice sank again.

On the platform, he walked and stared at his shoes. He didn't see them or he would have seen his socks. He hunted for words. He stood at the window and looked into the street for them.

"More than by any other means"—at last he was looking away from the window and speaking—"you can tell the moral condition of a country by the people it keeps in its slums." He searched the room and found her.

I should have sat at the back, she told herself, sinking lower in her seat.

When a wrinkled yellow sheet of paper fell from the platform to the floor, an eager student in the front row sprang up to snatch it. He also snatched the time to ask a question full of jagged, broken language. "Apposition to your formulation . . ." "ineluctable realization." Could this be what she was hearing? These broken pieces the student stuck together in rows with a pasty phrase, "as it were." Whenever the student had to take a breath he let go another drop of as-it-were glue to hold things together. Anzia thought of creeping back several rows while Dewey once more gazed through the window.

Anzia flung a look at the seats behind her. Students there were drawing portraits on the arm desks, and one or two had slumped into sleep. The truth was that Professor Dewey's lecture, to Anzia astonishment, was boring. That did not stop her from hanging on to every word she could catch. A man of about forty, dark-browed and stocky, gazed up from among the young graduate students. Dressed in an elegant striped suit, he twisted a fountain pen between his lips. When he felt her looking, he gave her a hard stare and clamped down on the pen with his teeth so that his heavy jaws bulged. Anzia felt she had been given a shove backward. This, she said to herself, is not a person who is here to learn what's moral. Beside him sat another man, somewhat younger, also stocky, though blond, and with coarse and thickened features. He too stared coldly when he felt her gaze, but more purposefully, as if to fix her in his mind. Another one who's not looking to learn right from wrong. Who are these men? Why are they here? she asked herself, but had no time to guess or imagine.

17

The society ladies began with *their* bottles of as-it-were glue. "But Professor Dewey, how can you as-it-were take away our as-it-were absolutes? Doesn't our civilization as-it-were depend on them?" Anzia wondered if as-it-were was like influenza, and you could catch it in a classroom.

His answer was simple and straight-out. "We know what isn't moral. Whatever keeps us from growth and change."

Still they went on. "How will society as-it-were survive?" Hadn't they heard him? Why were they so slow in understanding? They were smiling and flirtatious. The argument was a game for them. She couldn't bear their slowness! It was unfair that he who spoke with such plain words was not understood! She wanted to tear apart every one of the roses on their luscious hats and hand back bare stems. "Here you are, Mrs., no more as it were." A powerful inner force twisted her up from her seat and turned her around to face the ladies in the back.

"Don't you hear what he's been saying? Over and over? We *know*. Whatever keeps us from growth and change is wrong!" In the shocked silence that followed, she lowered her burning face over her notebook. If she could have grown invisible then, vanished forever, she would gladly have done it.

After class she waited inside her cage of shame, away from the others. Not to speak but to overhear him speak. She saw him look around. Then, astonished, saw him move toward her. The society ladies with their books gave way. "Will you wait, please, till I am done here?" Then he returned to his questioners.

Anzia had to sit again, looking at the notebook in her lap, the mutilated pencils whose leads she had broken through nervous dropping and tried to gnaw new points on. Was he going to tell her what she already knew, "You don't belong here"? She couldn't give up now, no matter how big a fool she made of herself.

The coarse-faced blond man who had sat alongside the dark-haired one, both glaring at her, leaned against a wall, surveying the room. The dark-haired man had already left. As she sat there, her head dizzy with a jumble of ideas about how she would defend herself against not belonging, the blond man came sauntering toward her. His grin, split across the width of his broad jaw, was not friendly.

"You like to make a commotion, don't you?"

I don't have to answer everybody who wears a suit, she told herself.

"No control," he said. "I saw that right away. It's a problem you people have."

Anger flicked through Anzia's chest and burnt up the feeling of shame. "Who is 'you people'? Who are you? Who was that man sitting next to you, dressed in such fancy clothes? The dark-haired man who looks like he could chew up a desk all by himself?"

The blond man feigned astonishment. "Don't you know him? Dr. Albert C. Barnes? The millionaire? The inventor of Argyrol, that swabs infected throats from sea to sea?"

Anzia's hand automatically flew to her own throat, as if to ward off sickness. "Why is this millionaire inventor mingling with mere students?"

"It so happens that Dewey's ideas on education are of interest to him. I don't expect you to understand what I'm saying. How would someone like you know anything about it? Dr. Barnes plans to educate the American public to principles of great art. He bought his paintings in Paris. He told me himself he got them for a song, those painters were starving. They're worth a fortune. He owns the greatest collection in America. He publishes books on art, too. They're available to the buying public. But I'll tell you something." He put his face a little closer to Anzia's. "The public will damn well have to stand on their heads before he'll let them in to look at those paintings. If he does let them in he may just kick their behinds for them, make them stick out their bums and take it. They can't just look all they want at painted naked women without paying up."

Anzia drew as far back in her chair as she could. "Who are you? Who do you kick?"

The blond man smiled with satisfaction. "I'm Marsh. I'm Dr. Barnes's assistant."

You're his flunky, Anzia thought. Your master kicks you, and you'd like to kick me.

Professor Dewey approached them. Marsh drifted away as unceremoniously as he had come. Anzia stood. When the professor came alongside, the pencils dropped from her grasp again. She rose from picking them up with a handsome flush on her velvety skin, fell into step, and walked with him from the class-room toward the open campus paths.

"When I burst out that way in class—!" Anzia began in an excited voice, eager to explain. Then she interrupted herself sadly. "I'm bursting out again. It's my curse. I can't suppress myself."

"Well." His words were as deliberate and slow as hers were quick. "Neither can . . ."

She had time to wonder how he would complete his sentence. Neither can I? Neither can my wife? Neither can—she was remembering the grinning Marsh—any of you people?

". . . a volcano or waterfall," he finished in a kind of drawl.

He combed his fingers through the panel of fine hair that fell across his brow, lifting it from his eyes. Only then could she tell—from his eyes, not his mustache-shielded lips—that he was smiling.

"I can't be patient—look how time is flying," she plunged on. "Already I'm nearly thirty!" (She knew she was some years past that, but gaps in immigrant papers allow some liberties, at least.)

"And I'm already nearly twice your age. I *must* be patient," he said.

A moment of memory rose up like a whale in the sea. Then it sank again, unknowable. What was it? Something to do with when he'd caught her, she thought. In his office. In her faint. In his arms. Whatever it was, it made the blood boom in her ears now.

There came between them such a silence that she had to wedge words into it. She asked, as if he were an ordinary person on her street, if he had children.

He nodded, but said that two were gone. "Two little ones. One nine, the other two years old. Some years ago, of course. Gordon and little Morris." She waited for an outburst, a lament. But after he gave out this terrible information, he only lifted his face a little and gazed with quiet sadness at the library dome.

"Is there—I don't know—some way . . . ?" They were wandering into a little grove of trees and bushes behind the walk. "How can I learn it . . . to speak like everybody in that room . . . with such coldness?" As soon as she said "coldness," the hot blood rushed to her face. "Can I ever learn that?"

His dark eyes could read the hardest books. She had expected fierce machines that ground up words, not these eyes, soft and shy, browsing for a moment in her gaze.

"Easily," he said. "Didn't you notice how many people know how? It's all they know." He stood silent for a while. Then, so low that she had to strain forward, "And I'm here like this. My armor's in place, all right. All my feelings shoved inside to save them. Can I unlearn that?"

Now he was following a pigeon's flight through the air and she wondered, What is he watching? It's not just a pigeon. The memory—the whale—suddenly broke through from its depths in shocking plainness. In that moment when she was in a half-faint in his arms, hadn't he leaned to her lips and kissed? Well, what else was it? Some effort to revive, like a lifeguard at a beach? Had she imagined it? If so, how could she feel, right now, the tingle of mustache hairs, the warm pressure of lips? Some impulse, it might have been, that startled and overcame him, like the one bringing him to the tormented question he had just asked.

He was looking at the sky and waiting for an answer. Which one could she give? "Easily," like him? She had no answer to a question she couldn't believe in. Or to the one he asked after that when he lowered his head a little, and his hair slipped over his forehead again so she couldn't see the expression in his eyes.

"Please, Anzia. Can you teach me?"

It startled her to think she knew him well enough to picture his pain.

3 ···≼

A Hat with Cherries

Now, only weeks after Anzia's faint, their relationship galloped ahead. Whether John's fingers had or had not pressed into her flesh—quick, surreptitious, boys let out into a school playground—whether his lips had or hadn't brushed against hers when she went limp, weak, does it matter? The temptation alone sends hot lava bubbling through the blood. Even the good man, knowing he mustn't pluck fruit from his neighbor's tree (to veer from volcanic to pastoral), savors fruit anyhow when it falls, ripe, into his hands.

Left to himself, John Dewey might dream, but not, of course, dream of doing such a thing. Anzia came into John's life: John talked of coming to her room. A case of classic awkwardness—the professor crossing the line. First he offers to take a kindly interest in the student, then he kindly offers to take the student. It's always the student's fault, of course. She's young, without knowledge of withholding, and eager to exploit her incredible luck with her hero-teacher. Anzia spilled her words, leaned her bosom too close, and behaved like an excitable ghetto girl. None of this made her terror less.

For days Anzia shakily prepared for his visit. Pulled bits of cloth from pushcarts to brighten the dark bed blanket and hide the wornness of the chair. The curtains she sewed herself, yellow cloth bought cheap to give a sunshine lie to the no-light window. After they were hung she twisted the material in her hands and rubbed it harshly against her face. She called herself a fool, not because the room was ugly, and he would see it, but because of his coming there at all. Haven't you had enough of love and how it wraps its feathers around your neck till you can't breathe? She was astonished to see how she was already growing used to thinking that he loved her.

This was how it began. They had been walking again after class. Marching bands and parades made such a din she could hardly think when he—she couldn't yet say "John"—mentioned a visit to her room. Neither of them spoke of the time before, when he asked if she would teach him. Teach him what? she wondered for the hundredth time. On God's earth, what could he have to learn?

The cherries dangling from her hat rose and bounced as they walked, in rhythm to the trumpet voice in the street singing the war song. "Over there!" I'd like to throw this hat over there, she thought. In a moment of joy and foolishness she had bought it. Why did you buy a hat? she demanded of herself now, again, lying on the bed and staring at the ceiling's cracks and stains. She shuddered, picturing its gaudy fruit, a last bit of the ghetto not yet squeezed from her soul.

In a nervous burst of words Anzia had said, "I've heard people talk about your views on the war."

"What do *you* think, Anzia?" They were by then sitting on a bench in Central Park, where she'd first eavesdropped on those views. When she leaned forward, the cherries on the hat brim tumbled forward with her, like brains spilling out.

"I'm too ignorant to think about it." She was punishing herself for the hat, though she had read and read. "I hear you discuss your writings on the war and I don't know anything about them. Or the magazines they're in. I hear you say 'Mill, neecha, can't.' Why can't they?" She suffered, hearing her own dumbbell dialogue, made even worse by the grave courtesy of his replies.

"They're stuck, that's why." A small smile started at a corner of his lips under the shielding mustache. "By God, they're stuck."

"My ignorance is a joke." She meant the hat.

"No, Anzia." He hurried to correct her impression. "Kant, you recall—"

"I can't recall can't when I can't know what it is."

Now he was reassuring. "You will. For you this will be like falling off a log."

Why was *that* a good thing? She was bruised from falling off too many logs.

"You're capable of every kind of learning. It's a joy to watch you." He tossed into the air a few golden balls of knowledge. She snatched what she could. A German philosopher named Kant—"K-A-N-T, Anzia"—had written about certain natural laws of being. John said these natural laws were called the Categorical Imperative, which Anzia in her nervousness (buzzing in the ears, constriction in the brain, booming in the blood) misheard as the Capitalist Incentive. She was astonished, therefore, to hear John add, "So the order from German higher-ups to torpedo even a ship full of women and children is carried out without hesitation. If only they could have read William James's *The Moral Equivalent of War* instead. Or cared less about following autocrats and more about experiencing freedom. Democracy can't win without a fight now."

John meant, Anzia knew, the sinking of the *Lusitania* and atrocities in Belgium. The German mind, John said, had mistranslated Kant's interesting idea about obeying a few natural laws into obedience in all things. He had just been putting an article together on that very subject. He was acquainting her with journals and periodicals by bringing her his own writing. In the few weeks since she had known him, he had shown her an astonishing output of essays published in *Atlantic Monthly*, *The Nation*, *Seven Arts*, *Dial*, *Child Labor Bulletin*, *The New Republic* and *International Journal of Ethics*. Struggling to wrestle her own words onto paper, she saw with something like fear the ease with which his prose poured itself onto the page. Once there, unfortunately, it seemed to clot like soap.

It was her own laws of being that weighed her down. Why can't you change faster? she said to them. It turned out it was the nation that was going to change.

"America will never be the same after this war," John said. "It all comes together—the raw work force we've been letting into the country for years, and industries going full blast at home while we fight a war on foreign soil. No one will call us a boardinghouse of aliens any more. America," he said with the familiar reflective lag in his voice, "will come out of this a world power."

He had not grown excited or loud. But she was startled to see him—such a gentle man—give so much of himself to the idea of war. Was this still another side of him? These bits of John kept poking through like pieces of a person ordinarily kept hidden under clothing. Suddenly John began to sing. In his flat, husky voice, singing!

"He hugged me and he kissed me
So hard he broke my jaw;
I could not speak to tell him
He forgot his mackinaw."

"I've only heard so far Beethoven," she blurted in shock and confusion, expecting anything he sang, if he sang at all, to be elevated. "But since the war they don't play it."

At first he burst out in a laugh. Then he crossed his arms and leaned back to look at her gravely. She thought a light like love lit up his eye, then scorned herself for thinking it. Because you're lonely you make up things.

"Experience teaches you everything you need to know, Anzia."

Wearing her hat, how could she also wear his laurels? "Your lectures are food and drink to me. But where's the table of learning to set them on? I haven't got it," she said in bitter reproach to herself.

"That's your blessing. Philosophers like to pretend reality is out there. Finished, once and for all. Waiting for us to touch it."

She heard that John was trying to teach her more about philosophy, but her brain went swimming again because now he was reaching out and touching the cherries on her hat. His voice sank again while he cupped a cluster of them in his palm. "We have the power to alter what's out there by responding in new ways. Who can live and not see the truth of it? Leaning back to gaze at reality is otiose."

He had used the word before and Anzia had looked it up. *Otiose.* It made her frantic to have forgotten its meaning. (When she looked it up again she saw—oh, God, yes—useless! Couldn't he have said so?)

"Remember my ignorance. Don't make my head spin with abstractions," she pleaded, leaning toward him on the bench.

He nodded. "Too much abstract-mindedness spoils my writing. My lectures put people to sleep."

"Oh, no!" At that moment she pictured the sleepers in the rows behind her at his lectures. "Give one little example only, and it will do wonders for my brain."

He stopped, reflected. Then: "Once there was a little boy named John."

Out of kindness, she thought, he is decreasing his size to a child's.

"This little boy named John liked to watch lumberjacks come into Burlington from the lumber camps. They went straight to the taverns, where women stood in doorways with their arms wide open. . . ."

She was watching as much as hearing. His small smile, his hair dropping into his eyes, and beneath it his brown clear gaze. She thought a smell of sweet grass and book leather came from him. It made her take deep breaths. What she thought of as his philosopher's furrow was making a deep vertical groove, as if memory cut literally and painfully into his flesh.

"The women called all the men Jack, and Jack is a nickname for John. It made the little boy very happy. He thought he was seeing the reunion of families. His father joked that the men were glad to get their mackinaws back. He sang the song about the logger lover. His mother never liked his father's jokes. Those were wicked men and women, she said. The little boy believed neither one. He believed his own two eyes, telling him how good it felt to the men when the women put their arms around them."

Anzia had already pictured his beginnings with envious eyes. His American birthplace was always snow-curtained. Cool. Clean. With the beautiful sparseness of New England villages, whose smoke climbed from the chimneys in clean narrow columns.

His father was keeper of a store never seen or imagined in the ghetto. Immaculate. The smells northern. Cold grains— buckwheat, oat, barley—each a universe sifting from wooden scoops. Hams, too, that forbidden food. Cloth-wrapped, cured of what ailed them, they dangled from hooks winter and summer and like corpses of Egyptian kings escaped corruption. Black-rind cheese wheels on the counter, ripened in the north-country climate and hard enough to ride wagons over rutted country roads. The white-haired gentleman behind the counter was his father, clever Yankee who composed the sign that hung before the shop: HAMS AND CIGARS, SMOKED AND UNSMOKED. The mother, delivered heart and soul to Jesus—"Are you *right* with Jesus?" John said she constantly asked, turning him away from such thoughts forever—Anzia never succeeded in picturing.

When at last she pulled off the hated hat and flung it on the bench, John reached out and drew it toward him. It climbed his knee, then his rumple-trousered thigh, then filled his lap with bright red cherries.

"The truth is"—his fingers played with the fruit—"there's only one thing in Burlington I feel enthusiasm for. Only the memory of those greetings between lumbermen and the women in the taverns. Even if it was rye whiskey and imminent departure that made their voices ring with so much joy. I felt their hearts were warm—"

He broke off, lifted her hand, pressed its palm to his lips.

Then, in a voice so low she had to bend nearer to hear, he asked, "May I visit you sometime at home? I'd like to be able to picture you there when we're apart."

She felt she'd been struck by one of those trees that fell outside Burlington. "It's just a room," she whispered in terror, "a tiny ugly room."

He was silent. Only those pain-filled eyes spoke.

That night she dreamed she was sinking into quicksand. An angel leaned from a mountaintop and let down a long scroll of writing. Just in time she caught hold and was lifted up, drawn inside the angel's wings. After waking, she still felt in her flesh that sensation of rising.

I've loved him, she thought, since the day he stuck out his arms to keep me from falling. That was when she twisted up the yellow curtains in her hands and wondered if there was still some way to keep him from her room. If he does come—she planned it after she flung herself down on her bed and lay there staring at cracks and stains in the ceiling—he'll find the bed covered not with rose petals but with manuscripts and books, too thorny and sharp to lie on.

So Anzia prepared for him, but all the thorns were sticking in her.

4

A Visit to the Lower East Side

Anzia kept pushing the visit away, John kept pulling it closer. He saw through her delays, and finally he pleaded.

"At least let me come and watch you teach. Every part of your life is important to me."

First come to my teaching, she translated, then to my bed? Is that where education will end? By means of the despised certificate already wrested from Teachers College, Anzia had been conducting her cooking classes for Lower East Side girls in the Henry Street Settlement House run by wealthy German-Jewish matrons. The humanitarian aim of this earlier wave of German-Jewish immigrants, now feeling comfortably assimilated to American life (not higher education at elite institutions, not politics, not society, not marriage, not clubs, not boards of corporations or the power-brokering philanthropic foundations, not medical schools or distinguished law firms, but everything else), was to upgrade this wave of Eastern-European Jewish immigrants, this assault on America of pogrom-battered refugees who reflected so poorly on those who'd come before. Self-serving the philanthropy may have been (in Federations, in B'nai B'riths, in Joint Distribution Committees, in Sisterhoods and Brotherhoods), but it achieved a positive good for the recipients. They flooded the settlement houses to perfect their skills and the educational alliances to improve their minds, and they flourished. In a few decades they outstripped their German-Jewish benefactors in creative energy, if not in manners.

When Anzia thought of writing ahead of time in her journal about John coming to her room (she knew that's where his visit to her class would end), the impossible became more so. What can I even write? She experimented anyway, trying accounts of varying futility and failure. The ceiling bulb shone on his blue and brown socks as his shoes came off? (How Chekhov said to write—describe the moonlight on the broken bottle in the gutter.) And then, sixty isn't twenty, or even thirty. Suppose his pent-up passion spilled out too quick and too soon? That would be the laundry side of romance! Afterward, she tore up those attempts. What had any of this to do with him?

Against husband and father she had developed the resistant strength families grant to those who escape them. She felt unable, or unwilling, to find the strength to refuse John. Yet she plotted how to refuse. She would lead him through the maze of the Lower East Side, and every sidewalk would fill him so full of sensation that he would reel away and forget her room.

When they got there, Anzia let John stand in the middle of it all for a minute, while it sank in. Vendors shouted wares— "Feesh!" "Wegables!" "*Viber, koyf!*"—wagon drivers sent oaths into the air, threatening throngs on foot with the hooves of horses. A child no more than nine trudged under a bundle of clothing parts like a little grandfather. John's boot heel skidded on a rotten pear that rolled from a pushcart. Anzia reached out, touched his arm to steady him, then pulled her hand away at once.

"Hester Street," she announced sternly. Fish heads and fruits rolled and splattered. A filthy stream poured along the gutters. "You see what a hell it is."

At the pavement, double rows of pushcarts lined the gutters hub to hub: then people, hip to hip. Even in autumn heat the women covered their heads with heavy cloths while they went about their business, their skirts sweeping the gutters. Men also dressed as if the only season they understood was winter: each with a dark jacket, however frayed, and a black-brimmed hat on his head—or a billed cap that gave him, above a bushy untrimmed beard, the look of a biblical sportsman.

Above this street throng was another throng. At each window, faces. On each fire escape, figures. This upper-level life, this second street, contemplated the one below. Anzia was suddenly in fear of seeing her father, though he seldom went into the street. He might be standing on one of those fire escapes, looking down at her.

All around them, Yiddish yielded up its passion. Anzia translated arguments, insults, pleas. John's ears took in short tragic stories that ended with bitter laughter, long comic ones that finished in heartfelt sobs.

Ludlow, Division, Rivington—she led him past the two-story tenements, back-to-back walkthroughs connected by air shafts that became chimneys for the devastating tenement fires.

At Washington Place and Greene Street, where the Triangle Shirtwaist Factory once stood, she pointed at the spot with an indignant finger.

"Doors to the fire stairs were locked against women stepping out for a breath of air. Hundreds of them burned up with their treadles and bobbins."

She felt ashamed of using a six-year-old tragedy to distract him, especially since he held out his arms in sympathy, as if she'd just told of the death of relatives. She stepped nimbly to one side and remarked that a man with a dark bowler hat and a cigar had passed behind a pushcart. She thought it might be the one in their class, the millionaire from Philadelphia. Or else, she said, it might have been his assistant, also in the class.

"Al Barnes?" John asked, astonished. "Or Harry Marsh— here?"

"Maybe I made a mistake," Anzia said shakily. "Anyway, whoever it was is gone now."

She wondered herself if she had really seen Barnes—or was it Barnes's assistant?—or invented one or the other to push away John's arms.

"They both make me uneasy," Anzia said. "I feel their dislike." The assistant, Harry Marsh, smoked cigars too and also wore a black bowler hat.

"I don't know much about Marsh," John said, "except that

he was once a boxer like Barnes. I suppose this makes him a valuable fellow to have around if you possess a fortune. I do know that Barnes is in some ways a rough-cut fellow, Anzia, but he struggled up through brains and gifts, like you. Now he's a benefactor to the world."

"Couldn't he have been a benefactor without making millions?"

"Barnes," John patiently explained, "invented a silver nitrate compound useful for anything from sore throat to simple disinfectant. Argyrol earns his fortune, it's honestly come by. I don't fault a man for not being a saint."

A saint was just what Anzia thought John might be himself, because of his habit of seeing good in so many people, including the scowling Dr. Barnes.

But when John reached for her hand, she found she required it to open the door of the settlement house, where they had finally arrived.

Forty girls stood at two long wooden tables, each at her own one-burner gas stove, each with a clean apron, hair bound in white cloth, hands carefully washed beforehand, according to the instructions of the settlement charity ladies.

While John took a chair Anzia faced the class and plucked a few eggs from the big wire basket.

"More important than eggs," she told the class, "is keeping the brain active during this mindless work of cooking."

Then while she broke, beat, splattered, she demonstrated the active brain: she recited by heart from Keats's "Ode to a Nightingale."

"Thou was not born for death, immortal Bird!
No hungry generations trod thee down—"

The cooking class began to giggle. Anzia ignored the poor girls, too ignorant yet to appreciate.

Clang! Clang! Clang! The heavy fork beat against the metal sides of the bowl. Above it Anzia shouted:

"The voice I hear this passing night was heard
In ancient days by emperor and clown . . ."

Fat sizzled in the pan. She raised her voice and recited louder:

"... *the self-same song that found a path*
Through the sad heart of Ruth, when, sick for home,
She stood in tears amid the alien corn."

The lower East Side girls noticed it before Anzia—the eggs burning black—and reacted, some with gasps and some with bold laughter. Luckily, Anzia had read John's ideas on the importance of experience for the student.

"Feel free to experiment," she said in a loud voice, as if this had all been planned.

They dropped, broke, burned eggs, and at last cleared out.

Slowly John rose from his chair and came toward her.

"I can't be less than honest with you. You're a god-awful cooking teacher."

"Learn from experience, you wrote!" She defended herself with his own ideas, though she understood them better than she practiced: indifference isn't experience; chaos isn't experiment.

Absently, lost in reflection, he took up one egg, then two, cracking them against the pan as if to test for himself the possibilities in this encounter with eggs.

Their insides slipped out and lay in the pan like the breasts of a woman reclining, the soft padded circles fallen back against her body. They looked at him. They hissed in their butter.

What will you do now?

His dark eyes searched her face. *Now*, she thought. He'll ask to come to my room. I'll show him the Eldridge Street Synagogue instead.

Once more she swept them into the dense-packed streets. On East Broadway they passed a tall tan building. The clock under its roof told the time, three o'clock. Plaques on its façade spelled MARX, ENGELS.

"That's the home of the *Jewish Daily Forward*, the Yiddish paper that boasts a million readers, and Abraham Cahan who is its editor will not publish my stories."

"He will." John turned as if to comfort with an embrace. The arm of his jacket seemed to lift by itself, a rumpled wing.

She hurried him on. Orchard and Canal. Jarmulowsky's Bank and the sweatshops above it where she'd worked.

"They sweated me so well"—she treated John to the blackest ghetto humor—"I was too tired at night to look for the job I wanted, at the Triangle Shirtwaist Factory. Otherwise I could have had the privilege of working and dying there too."

He curled his long-fingered hand around the back of his neck. "Thank God you didn't."

Shouts and curses exploded around them. A loaded pushcart overturned, spattering them with pulp. Anzia drew back, but John stood his ground amid the fruit, its smell fermenting in their nostrils. He joined the pushcart owner in scooping apples from the ground. When he had wiped his hands on his handkerchief he came toward Anzia.

She remarked that now she saw two black bowler hats and two cigars passing behind a pushcart filled with bananas. "There!"

To her astonishment, Barnes himself, a large, stocky man, really did come through the throngs with his assistant, Harry Marsh. They were both smoking cigars, but only Barnes's black bowler hat was shoved forward slightly over his somber glare.

"It *is* you, Al!" John said.

Harry Marsh let loose his rapid-fire speech, upon which Barnes's deep slow tones at times descended like a gavel. "Dr. Barnes was over at a painter's studio looking at some work," Marsh began quickly. "I browsed along here till we could meet. . . ."

How could I have imagined that Marsh was spying on us for his master? In self-reproach, Anzia reminded herself of what she so far knew about Barnes. He had grown up in a slum, the more shaming because it was a slum for Americans, not an immigrant one. That outlying section of Philadelphia was known as the Neck, where the poorest families lived in squatters' shacks pitched in unhealthy marshlands, and where the children who played among the reeds were more dangerous, it was rumored among respectable Philadelphians, than the marsh rats. It was a fascination to Anzia, when she learned of Barnes's origins, to wonder why he might in turn have rescued Harry Marsh, the younger man from the Neck. Was it because Marsh's name made a kind of lasting memento to everything Barnes had overcome?

Barnes had shown intelligence and quickness, had earned

recognition from teachers and scholarship money to study chemistry in Germany. He had come home a conquerer of his fate and, soon, inventor of the money-making formula, Argyrol. Though there, too, rat rumors clung to him. Some said that Barnes had caused his German-born inventor-partner to be deported, or else that Barnes had in some way got rid of him, paid him off perhaps, leaving Barnes in sole command of his patent and financial kingdom.

All this Anzia gleaned from corridor gossip about the glum-faced millionaire. She also heard that Barnes's student days in Europe provided him with a center from which to make forays into France, where he learned about paintings that could be bought for the pittance he was so fond of spending on art. A different world. Why should any of this make Marsh or Barnes want to spy on John and her?

"Anzia saw you way before I did," John said to Barnes, proud of her.

Barnes expelled a short laugh from under his bowler. "Slum brats develop extra senses."

John looked with warm appreciation at Anzia and Barnes, his slum friends who had changed so spectacularly that they had burst out of themselves. "What could be more sensible?"

They went on walking. Barnes and Marsh on one side of John, Anzia on the other.

"How was it to grow up in such richness?" John bent his brow to Anzia like a sheet of fresh paper to write on.

Richness hadn't occurred to her. But she had enough to tell, some stories true, others an imagining of the truth. From the corner of her eye she saw, and pretended not to see, Barnes's assistant making strange faces. Barnes kept his gaze stolidly ahead, but Marsh pushed his lips over to one side and ran his forefinger back and forth beneath his nose as if he couldn't stand the smell of something. Anzia plunged in anyway, mixing up the plots of all the stories she meant to write about the Lower East Side, bits of life mingled with bits of invention. She stumbled on the cobblestones. It was hard to make the words come out, as if Barnes or his assistant held a hand over her mouth.

". . . but when this woman's children got rich and moved her uptown away from her slum, she drowned in loneliness and separation from her own kind."

Marsh dragged down the corners of his mouth with his fingers. He stuck out his tongue like a devil. Anzia couldn't believe that John didn't see. She was sure by now the faces had something to do with her, but she went on anyway.

She told how she had been a peddler as a child, for a few cents one rainy day renting a heavy pushcart. Schlomo the fruit peddler let her have apples and bananas because he thought business would not be good. When she ran home and poured her pennies on the table, her mother's wailing filled the dark kitchen. " 'God in heaven! Was it for this I brought forth children?' But my father," she went on, eyes half closed in a delicious composing trance, not caring if Barnes heard it too, "thought it right that I should bring in pennies. That my marriage should be a matter of his will. I had to break away, fight him off. 'Hurricane and destruction,' he called me. 'Red-haired disease.' "

The moment John left them to buy pears from a pushcart, Marsh turned to Anzia. "That's right, play it to the hilt!" he said in an outraged voice. "The genius from the lower depths." He leaned his head close to her and cried out bitterly, "Let me tell you, Dr. Barnes is the genius from the lower depths!"

"That's enough," said Barnes, tracing figures on the ground with his stick, his voice deep and remote as if it came from somewhere else.

Anzia said she wasn't fighting anyone for the honor.

"You don't mind at all! You walk around telling yourself lies and then write them down. One of these days you'll tell lies about us. What you call *stories*," Marsh taunted her.

"That's enough. I won't be demeaned!" Barnes said in a rage.

As soon as John returned, Barnes with a slight movement seemed to block his path. Elegant in his keenly pressed suit, his bowler, his walking stick and gold vest chain, he asked, "Going uptown, Jack? My car's only a block or two away. I'll give you a lift."

"Why . . . in that case . . ."—John seemed barely able to answer—"then . . . I suppose—"

If Barnes had rescued her, what was this pang she felt as John prepared to go? Admit that you wouldn't have kept him forever from your room, she told herself.

John gave her the bag of pears. She held out to him the string of figs they'd bought along the way. He took them into his hand, put a fig to his lips, bit through its tough skin, and chewed at the pith.

As they walked toward the car she heard Barnes say, "Those'll make you crap, Jack!"

She fell into tormented dialogue with herself. If Barnes is what I think, then how can John, who knows everything, not know that? Is it John's goodness that makes him blind? Or is it ghetto darkness that twists my vision? Which? What?

Why should a character (even one based on real life and not entirely, so to say, the writer's responsibility) flail around in confusion because she had no access to insights all around her? Freud's views were already widely published. But Dewey did not find Freud a fruitful study. Dewey did not care for introspection. The more he looked inward at conflicting selves, the less he wanted to see. Within that kindly, earnest, bland family man and absentminded professor he'd already encountered the man of pent-up passion, the would-be adulterer. And maybe, after all, Barnes himself? Another psyche doctor whose work Anzia could have consulted had she known of it, C. G. Jung, might have shown that Barnes was the shadow figure to John's figure of light. The bad boy, who fascinates the boy who doesn't disobey, familiar to every schoolyard. What is absent from experience is also present.

Social ills and the hearty, healthy energy of pitching into their amelioration, these were what Dewey told Anzia he discerned were his dish. Yet—he admitted it—word had come to his ears that Freud admired him, calling Dewey the one man in America worth reading. Dewey, said Freud, had hit upon a great truth about the human mind: it is from start to finish incapable of separating itself from its own experience and can build only upon that.

After all this can I come up with answers, for Anzia's sake, to her painful questions? Why Dewey not only put up with Barnes but enjoyed his company and allowed himself to remain blind to Barnes's treatment of others? I can't (I K-A-N-T) though I would like to. I struggle now with these simple and unfamiliar novelist's tools. Must I become a psychologist too? Worse yet, a philosopher? Some of you will come up with better answers of your own.

I would have liked to find answers, both for Anzia's sake and for the sake of those late-sixties days when, as an eager young social worker and soup-bringer to the bedrooms of the old, I found myself a sometime confidante of Anzia, then (as I figure) in her eighties, who never forgot a syllable spoken to her or recounted it, I suspect, unchanged. I must have caught her storytelling fever, if not her gift. It all went smoldering in my brain, erupting at last when I learned that Dewey's buried poems had finally flung open their coffin, still bleeding, like something in a story by Edgar Allan Poe.

The young graduate students flocked to Anzia in those days, prospecting in literature for their roots. They crowded Anzia's small room in the Hebrew Home for the Aged on the sad Upper West Side in the days before its renewal. There she narrowed her eyes, at once merged with the young woman shut up inside the old one, and announced, "What's there to fear in dying? We already meet it when we're young. The end of a love tastes of death." Who? they all wondered. Who does she mean? Who were the John Morrows the Henry Bakers of her books? The mystery, in those days, was still sealed in the archives. I never learned the truth of it from her.

That day on the Lower East Side, tasting all the sweetness of a beginning, Anzia was asking herself, Who? Who are these men—John? Barnes? Marsh? Why is life so much like the silver nitrate compound Barnes claims to have invented, both a poison and a medication? She brought her confusions back to her writing and her room, where she took comfort in cradling John's pear in her palm.

5

"Fiery Kisses of Your Lips"

If you saw a cup filled with water from the ocean, would you picture whales and algae, storms and drowned people?

John brought such a cup of ocean to Anzia's room—his quiet shyness, in which all his passion was imprisoned. He stood there, still as Sargasso, his back pressed against her door.

The smell of the scorched kettle seared the air around them. She had meant to make tea.

His jacket pockets were bumpy with magazines, and as he leaned against the door they pushed forward mutely. Anzia leaned for support against the table she used as desk.

When the smell of the boiled-out kettle reached her, she laughed shakily and said, "My cooking class."

From the corridor came shouts of a shameful quarrel. The odor of boiling fish mingled with the smell of the scorched kettle.

"Are those"—she tried to cut into the block of marble that held them fast—"for me?"

He began to beat his bulging pockets as though he'd forgotten to bring her the periodicals.

"Would you like"—it was some word she wanted, not this pantomime—"a glass of tea?"

He shook his head no but his lips parted; he looked parched with thirst. "What more does anyone need?" Finally he was speaking. "A desk. A chair." He moved toward her. The last in his inventory of her room, "A bed," buried itself in his mouth at her breast.

The fur robes she'd seen through the windows of the motorcars of the rich were nothing compared to the luxury of holding him. All the same, she had to wrench away and run to the window to look out. She thought she heard among the cries in the street the summons of bad news. She thought she heard her own name.

Maybe I myself am calling it?

The sight of a black-hatted figure standing motionless beneath the fire escape made her think of the two men, Barnes and Marsh. Was this figure one of them? Would either one have followed so far as her doorstep? As if by accident, she brushed her hand against a small, tired plant that drooped its leaves in a pot on the windowsill. She watched it fall and land on the stranger's arm. The figure beneath the fire escape threw the other arm over to nurse the struck one, staggering a little. Then he looked up, shouting curses in Yiddish. She saw with relief that it was neither Harry Marsh nor Albert Barnes.

You're headed for the insane asylum, she told herself severely.

She slammed the window shut and threw her black wool shawl over the curtain rod for good measure. The room darkened.

"Was that neighbors?"

She said yes, to be done with it.

"The intimacy here! My colleagues who have a romance going with small towns in Vermont should know of this."

It was only embarrassment about the broken-into moment. They soon moved toward her bed, where the last light lay. . . .

What she recorded in her journal afterward was nothing at all like what she thought she would write. It seemed to her that John's flesh rose up with the wisdom of Solomon. Even his long toes, she thought, knew Aristotle.

•　　•　　•

When John began to write his poems and shyly show them to

her, Anzia wasn't at all surprised that Swinburne, that poet of hot passions, was his model. One began:

The fiery kisses of your lips
Scourge my mouth
And I taste the blood of life. . . .

"For you," John said, flushing crimson. "Look what you've given me."

Soon after, Anzia felt a strong need to catch a glimpse of Alice, who sometimes visited John's office.

"I might never have written if not for Alice," John said.

It was Alice who needed to have books spill from his pen. John's favorite place for his writing was the garbage. The wastebasket was always full. He liked the passage of ideas through his brain, but was indifferent to them afterward. He disliked the dryness and colorlessness of his language and could never bear to reread it.

"How can you be disgusted with your words?" Anzia asked. "They're like your own heartbeat!"

"Disgust with myself is more like it," John answered.

She understood this was long-standing.

Adding to everything now, former colleagues and friends had denounced him for deserting the pacifists. There was also domestic misery. Alice was melancholy. She had till now always worked with John, contributing ideas to his books, as well as typing his manuscripts. She had taught alongside him in The Chicago School's experimental classes, famous throughout the country. But New York and Columbia University had no place for her. She had to pour her own ambition into John. In his office she cried "Waste!" at the accumulation of crumpled yellow balls in the basket.

Barnes had gotten to his feet one day in the midst of John's lecture and walked to where a woman waited in the doorway. Her hat was black, shaped like an upside-down pot without ornament. Gray bands of hair showed beneath. Her features were small and at that moment so controlled as to be without expression. Her white shirtwaisted bust sagged into a stout waistband. Barnes led her—why was it everything he did seemed exaggerated and mocking?—toward a seat at the front. Silently she shook off his arm and walked on, taking a chair on the aisle midway toward the back. From there she turned a stern face toward John, who had noticed nothing.

Anzia began to shake. She had never before seen the woman who entered. But the idea took hold of her. This was Alice. Because of the lost children Anzia could forgive her anything, even for being John's wife.

But on the day of looking for Alice, the person she saw instead was William Dow, John's assistant, whose desk was in an outer office. He was just leaving with John's full wastebasket cradled in his arms. Anzia followed to see where he went.

Dow walked with a leg-shortened limp, one shoe set over a base as high as its boot top. At a safe distance down the marble corridor, Anzia followed the irregular blows of his tread, like her own excited heartbeat. It was a long corridor, and it ended in another office on whose door was painted the golden title LIBRARY CURATOR. The door was only half open, but when the curator saw Dow he rushed into the hall.

"You weren't"—pointing at the wastebasket—"about to throw that out!"

"If I were would I have come past your place?"

The curator was a man whose shirt collar was starched to stone, his tulip-cut jacket pressed as stiff as a keepsake flower. His collector's nose was collected tight inside the pincher of his spectacles. He acted like a spy. After a few days, dodging and eavesdropping, Anzia discovered what the conspiracy was about.

At the end of each day, or when the basket overflowed, the curator, with Dow's help but without John's knowledge, picked through the wastebasket, salvaging for the archives. The dignified curator and Bill Dow seemed to agree that the treasure they rescued was worth the deception.

Anzia eavesdropped day after day (taking endless drinks of water from the hall fountain) and learned of the curator's dedication to John's manure balls of yellow paper.

"I hate to think about going on vacation, Bill," said the curator to John's assistant. "He might be working in his office when you and I are both away. Think of the loss!"

After the transfer, the curator flattened every scrap into a large box to be stored away in the archives of Butler Library.

On especially thoughtful days, the wastebasket could over-flow by noon. Sometimes John forgot that Dow had disappeared with a full one, and went on tossing crumpled yellow sheets at the spot where the basket had been. That had happened the day Anzia burst in. Suddenly aware of the mess he'd made, John had been on his knees scooping it up.

Anzia had already smoothed out a few of these scraps her-self when no one was looking. "Art is the true cathexis of thought and feeling," she read. After she looked up "cathexis" and learned it was a word for deep connection, she carried it like honey on her tongue.

Another time, astonishment made her drop a scrap on the floor instead of back in the basket before she slipped away. *Sex is the impulse that drives thought,* she read. She didn't know then that others saw these things too.

It was clear that Alice had no idea what was going on. Aside from Dow and the curator, Anzia told herself, I am the only one.

Anzia began a new story. A woman rejected immigrant life and fell in love with a distinguished Gentile. But she couldn't altogether give up the old ways or enter the new life either. To write a story about a person paralyzed between two worlds and not also paralyze the story was the hardest thing Anzia had tried yet.

One evening the landlady knocked at the door and handed over a large envelope delivered by messenger. Anzia was sure it would be from John and tore it open excitedly. The sight of her own manuscript killed her joy. Still, the editor had taken the trouble to include a lengthy letter. A glance at the bottom showed it was signed by Abraham Cahan himself.

My dear Anzia:

With regret I return to you this newest story. As I have already told you, no doubt too many times, your work suffers from narrowness. Always you write about female domestic matters. Where is the labor move-ment? Where is the Russian Revolution? Where is war and its socioeconomic causes?

And of course you write about the Mysterious Stranger, the lover. By the way, who is or was he? I assume a real person because the obsession is real. I can count four or five different names in your stories. Frank Baker, John Morrow, and all the others add up to the same man. You call your heroines by different names—Fanya, Sheynah, Hanneh Breineh—but they are all the same woman.

Speaking as Editor of the *Forward*, I can tell you that this obsession stunts your work. It does not grow. Speaking as a friend, I tell you the same thing. Speaking as originator and Editor of *Bintel Brief*, into which the whole world pours its Jewish heartache, I invite you to tell me who is this goy who has taken over your life. A great lawyer? Man of letters? President of a college? Would I know him? I am not a shockable man. A hundred priests hearing confession all day have not heard more than I. I take it all with equanimity. I am like the rabbis of old to whom an unkosher chicken and an adulterous affair were alike matters for impersonal judgment.

If I could advise a pious woman who fell in love with the boarder and begged me to tell which of her twelve kiddies she should take along when she ran off with him, I can advise you. I will advise, my dear Anzia, what is best for your work. So tell me, who is this man? This John Morrow, Frank Baker, et al., this God-like creature that none of our Jewish intellectuals can approach in your eyes.

Perhaps I already suspect. You could reveal just his initials. The editor of *Bintel Brief* knows how to guard secrets. I have turned into a rabbinical court of one here on the *Forvitz*. Haven't you noticed how merciful I am to those who write for advice? And nobody has to bring gifts or pay tribute. All that is required is to spend a few pennies for the newspaper.

To you I offer free advice, without charging even one penny. Write me the name of this ideal man, this "intellectual, sensitive, caring"—I am picking out only a few of the adjectives in your stories. Write me who is this messianic goy and I will liberate you from the obsession that keeps your imagination chained to a single theme: Jewish Cinderella, girl from the ghetto burning to become an American who meets Prince Charming . . . enough! You and I both know this story by heart. As we know that in America in this beginning twentieth century the Happy Ending is not so 100 percent sure as in those creepy Black Forest stories collected by the Grimm Brothers. And who could prove the happiness of the lovers anyway? No witnesses. Happy-ever-after always took place offstage. If you ask me, as soon as the Germans got Cinderella off the page, her "happy ending" was—they murdered her. Besides, is the melting pot of lovers any better than of groups? Do your Jewish Cinderellas want to be melted down and disappear?

Sincerely yours,
Abraham Cahan

Anzia sent back a note.

Dear *Bintel Brief* Editor:

Thank you for such a long letter. You sound as if you are very curious about things you think might have happened in my life. In some ways, your letter suffers from this obsession. Where is the power of the imagination? Besides, I only wanted you to publish my story, not the contents of my wastebasket.

Bravado faded as soon as the letter was mailed. There was her story still unwanted on the table. Yet things were no longer the same. In John's arms she could also say, "A desk. A chair. A bed. What more does anyone need?" Even Barnes's millions couldn't match the richness.

6 ···≺

An American from
the Other Side

As spring neared, John worried about summer. He was expected to stay on the family farm in Huntington, Long Island,
where some of his children would be living. He'd be required to
spend time in San Francisco, where Alice was scheduled to visit
with one of their daughters. He wanted to escape all that.

Anzia's notion was to sit in her room and read and write till
John came back. He had seen to it that the bursar charged her
no tuition, and she had managed to save enough to live sparely
till the fall. Then they'd return to Columbia and one another.
But John said he'd made up his mind that by one means or another they would not be separated.

"A project of some sort." He worried aloud to her. "What
can it be, Anzia? A real project, something that will demand
time, take me away from Alice's summer plans, and bring you
and me together somewhere." He pulled and chewed at his mustache as if a second brain hid behind it and he was working it to
death. In class, as if to illustrate how painfully he searched for
a plan, his words came more slowly than ever. "There are people . . . who can never dare to . . . remove a finger from the
dike . . . of personality. . . ."

During one lecture he looked through the window for a long

time. Later he told Anzia he had noticed something while thinking things through. Two dogs on the loose, sniffing beneath one
another's tails. They could read private parts like intimate love
letters. Self-exposure for them was pleasure. Why had human
beings gone so far from their animal condition?

A fine thing if we'd stayed with the animals, Anzia thought.
But she understood what all that meant to him.

John invited Anzia to the Faculty Dining Room where he
lunched with his colleagues. The uniformed guard at the door
was instructed to admit her. It was a reckless act for both of
them. Still, she went. Why wouldn't she want to see? But fright
kept her pacing the hallway until half an hour had gone by.

Finally Anzia entered the dining hall. The circle of professors rose in their places around the table. Fragrant red roses
filled a vase inside a ring of silver coffeepots. Anzia saw with
relief that the eating was over. But the agony of introductions
still had to be endured.

"Professor Franz Boas here, of the Anthropology Department, keeps us connected to the apes," John said. All Anzia
knew was what she could see: a clever-looking man who watched
her curiously out of light-colored eyes. While he bowed, she
thought, Apes? and wondered, if she pushed back his sleeve,
whether she would find his arm pelted with fur.

Next came someone John said was "In history. Beard." Yes,
Anzia nodded politely to show she could see he was growing
one, though John only meant to indicate the great Charles Beard,
who was soon going to withdraw his friendship anyway, because
of Dewey's changed position from pacifist to supporter of America's intervention in the war. The supposed beard-grower bowed
slightly, while a tangle of frowns sprouted on his forehead. "And
F. J. Woodbridge." John was flipping his thumb in the direction
of each man as he spoke, to give an informal touch to everything. "We grope in the philosophical dark together."

When John said her name he added, "A writer we'll be
hearing from soon." All he'd seen was her sketch about her sister's trip to the charity vacation house, but he had tried to
transform her so that she could breathe among equals. She was
not, in any case, breathing well at all, and when she was served
coffee from one of the silver pots, she choked on her first sip
and gave up the thought of any others.

John launched into an anecdote. "Someone's been telling us a joke that traveled uptown from your part of the world. Burt and Leon comedy team, was that it?" He looked around the table, but the professors kept their eyes in their coffee cups. "It goes like this. Fifth Avenue swell to immigrant Ike, 'Are you a foreigner?' 'Who, me? Nah, I'm an American from de odder side.' " John's New England ear had not managed to catch the tone of Lower East Side Ike. The professors, who had laughed the first time around, were not tempted to laugh now, nor was Anzia. There was a general silence. Slowly, John repeated, "The other side. Of ourselves, I think Ike means. Of ourselves. . . ." He lapsed into a lengthy silent staring in the direction of a distant chandelier.

What did John see, Anzia asked herself for the thousandth time, when he stared off into space like that? Was it the other side of himself he was staring into? The place where mind couldn't go and only feelings could reach? She knew by now she was firmly placed in John's other side of himself. Was Barnes there too? Barnes showed passionate feelings, even if not the kind John wanted for himself—they were mostly growls and grudges. Now she had a frightening image to contend with: John's other side was a kind of clean, bare room, and she, Anzia, was in it, filling it with her passion like hot colors, the way she'd tried to fill her own poor room, or the way a painter might work on a cold white canvas. But Barnes was in it too.

The professors were exchanging looks, as if they knew that John was off on one of his long mental journeys and might not be back before the end of lunch. One by one they quietly excused themselves from the table. John returned from whatever place his musing had taken him to. He didn't seem surprised to find that he and Anzia were alone at the table. He grasped her hand—"We must think of some way!"—and shook it violently, without seeming to realize.

It had become their pattern to visit her room after class. The luxury of a rattling taxicab all the way downtown. This time, instead, John led them back to his colleagues' offices. Without a word, he suddenly left her and dashed down the hall, long legs scissoring swiftly, tie flying back over one shoulder. An undone bootlace rattled on the marble floor of the corridor. Anzia followed, wondering if strain had demented him. He was

shoving open an office door marked ANTHROPOLOGY DEPART-
MENT.

"Boas, I'm a fool!" John said. "The one thing I should have
asked—are there any projects? My students need summer work.
Trips? Fieldwork anywhere? Borneo? Splendid students!"

Anzia peeked around from behind John. Would Boas, in the
privacy of his office, have grown shaggy or be caught eating a
banana?

Professor Boas's light-eyed gaze in turn traveled back past
John to Anzia. "I gather you prefer the remote location?"

"Remote would be just right—yes! But I won't say no to
near at hand."

"I'll keep it in mind, John. Borneo? Samoa? Something may
be coming up."

"I'd be grateful," said John, turning away with a battered
look that made his friend Boas peer after him anxiously.

And later, to Anzia on her bed, "A project somewhere."
John groaned. "There must be!"

Thinking of the joke John told, Anzia remembered one in
Yiddish: "When a poor man eats a chicken, one of them is sick."
And when a famous American declares love for a poor immigrant, is one of them, she asked herself, having a nervous
breakdown?

Along Columbia's paths, shrubs were beginning to show birth
buds and redden the air. Birds sang, marble columns gleamed.
Alma Mater broadened her lap on Low Library steps while she
held up a cold torch with one hand and beckoned stonily with
the other. On the wide plaza at the base of the flowing steps,
their threesome stood in the perfumed air.

A few months before, Anzia had run here as hard as she
could. Now she wanted to run the other way.

"Over by the river in Philadelphia," Barnes was telling John,
calling him Jack. "Polishtown. They don't mix, don't mingle.
America's a stopping place for them. Back to the old country,
they think, Jack, the old ways after the war." He was dressed,
as always, in dark, elegant clothing, his manner as stiff and in-
timidating as John's was informal and easy.

Anzia bent to retrieve a paper someone had dropped on the
path. There was writing on it, notes from a class. Some student

might be frantic at this moment, searching for the missing page. Anzia stared as if to read an answer to the question that buzzed like an early spring fly in her brain: How could John and Barnes be friends?

Barnes kept on, his voice deep and heavy. "The Poles hate change, Jack. Clannish."

Did he say that about her too? Clannish? Hates change?

"Led by that piano tickler," said Barnes. "Paderewski."

After that came John's voice, reflective and calm but strained in a way familiar to her from that first day, when she thought, He needs me.

"There must be democratic factions there too, Al. Have to be." And then, offhand, as if John hadn't searched for something like this for weeks, though his voice cracked a little on it: "We ought to investigate, Al. Make it a summer's study."

She wished he would take it back. The next minute she asked herself, How *can* he, if everything we are and do leads to the next stage? Make the best use of things you can—on the one hand, on the other hand. That was it. Pragmatism. John's idea of how we think and learn. He said she was born knowing it. On the one hand she was, on the other she wasn't. She knew what he hoped for. Make our minutes mountaintops that pull us higher. Skip over them like rams. But through Barnes? His face was broad and powerful, his dark thick brows rushed together. Oh, yes, rams, she thought—*battering* rams.

"Will you start us off, Al? Get us some funding for a Philadelphia project?" John's voice was going hoarse now. "Then we'll see if Wilson wants us to go on. We'll contribute a study on why some immigrant groups don't integrate into the country—a study for peacetime America."

"A house for your crew in Polishtown. That's what you'd like, is it, Jack?" Barnes said he'd scout around before his next return to New York. He suggested a few students for the project. He left out Anzia.

John gave her a look. Don't mind this, the look said. He waved a hand as if introducing Anzia for the first time. As if she and Barnes had not sat together in John's classroom for months, with Harry Marsh watching everything.

"Anzia is someone who knows Polish as well as immigrant

life," John said. Then he added fervently, "Indispensable for our needs. Don't you see, Al?"

Barnes was rolling his cigar. Narrowing his eyes, as if the smoke made him. His wide mouth opened in a laugh.

"I see it now, Jack. Indispensable. Very good. I'll go to work. Count on me."

A vein in Barnes's temple swelled. His voice turned almost soft.

"And I'll be, Jack, honored if you'd visit. If you will. To see the collection. Matisse. Cézanne. Renoir. Those names mean nothing to the American public now. But I will make them mean. I've got no intention of throwing open the museum doors, Jack. They'll crawl to get in. Beg on bended knee."

"The American public will be in your debt, Al." John wasn't listening. Anzia could always tell. He withdrew to the back of his head. His eyes were like brown isinglass. Anzia thought he might be in her room now. On her flowered spread on the floor, with her, telling himself that the dingy rays that tilted over them were dappling love with springtime light.

"I may have to hack off thumbs at the door for admission fees, Jack."

She could tell John wasn't listening. She decided it would be best if she didn't either, and returned to her buzzing fly. How could they be friends? But since they were, could John be who she thought he was? Since Barnes was earnestly looking at John, and John was settling inside his brain, she felt she could freely examine the matter. John's handsome face retreated into shyness. Barnes's jutted into the world like a dare. Even their shapes were a contrast: John wiry and thin, Barnes broad and thick and dangerous-looking. The eyes, too: John's were a clear, soft brown. With Barnes you didn't think of iris, velvet flower-part. The contracted dots were hard as flint, cold as the black buttons Anzia used to sew on pants.

She saw in Barnes some upside-down image of John, as if reflected in a trick mirror. How can they be friends? she asked herself for the hundredth time. *Why* are they friends? Each time she answered a different way and was never satisfied. She tried once more. She could see without trouble why Barnes, with his bitter view of the world, would want to be near John, who saw the best in everyone. John's idea about democracy, that each human being, of whatever background, possessed a rich source of wisdom through personal experience, would attract a man like Barnes too. Barnes liked the *idea* of democracy. His arrogance never allowed him to mingle with the world the way John did, unless the world was willing to declare itself undemocratically inferior.

But why did John *enjoy* Barnes so much? (Who can prevent Anzia from worrying this question over and over?) Was it really because John's bringing up had in fact been a pushing down, and everything pushed down, long ago put severely away from himself, now surfaced in Barnes?

"So it's settled." John's voice—the mild, gentle, good-man's voice—suddenly broke forth. It was jubilant. He had been figuring things out during his silence. "Philadelphia. Where we'll be this summer."

You worry for nothing, Anzia told herself. Pay attention to your fears, she promptly replied to that. Back and forth, the argument in her head. On the one hand, on the other hand.

In the classroom, John's eyes found her in her seat. A wire of light seemed to connect them, a column, a beam, a ray of something. They were at opposite ends of what flared and vibrated between them. If he needs me to go I'll go, she decided. How simple it was, after all.

"This," John said. "What do we understand by 'this'? 'Take this message to President Wilson' is plain. But if a man comes into a room, points to nothing, and says, 'This is all a man needs,' we ask, 'What on earth is *this?*' "

What on earth is this? Anzia echoed. This idea to go to Philadelphia?

John's voice trailed off in thought. He stopped, paced, stood at the window, and looked out. After a moment, he went on. " 'My heart is bursting,' says the man. 'I cannot contain all this.' "

My heart is bursting, Anzia whispered into her notebook. I can't contain this. Go to Philadelphia or not?

"This. . . ." John's voice started up again. "First the sounds of 't' and 'h' must merge, unlooked-for coupling. . . ." His words came not so much to her ears. They seemed to slide past her skin and burn like rope. "Then the 'ih' sound," John said, "as up from the gut as any groan. Then 's-s-s-s,' the long sigh of ex-pelled relief."

Anzia pushed at her pencil and broke it. John gazed again through the window and murmured, "I think I have made this matter of 'this' a little clearer to myself." He seemed seized by fresh ideas, about to begin again. But a bell sounded down the hall, and the class scrambled out in relief.

Anzia's name was called. She stayed with the handful of students assembled. Emmet Trumbull, Irving Bitman—whose "as-it-were's" had glued together those long syllables that frightened Anzia on her first day—and Ellen Wright, the only other woman, who from the beginning had skittered her glance away from Anzia whenever their eyes met. Anzia marveled at the look of joy on their faces when John told them they had been picked for the project. They could not believe in their good luck! All of them eager, jumping at the chance to work with the Pol-ish community in Philadelphia next summer. What's wrong with me? she asked herself. Why do only I hold back?

She wanted to say she couldn't go. But John's gaze, full of hope, turned in her direction, and she said nothing. They had no moment to talk alone. John was called to a meeting. He left, the others followed, and soon only Anzia was still there, strag-gling toward the door. She heard a sound, a kind of imitation-polite cough: "Ahem! Ahem!"

She turned to see Albert Barnes. He was big and dark. All winter he had worn a thick coat with a fur collar. He looked like some powerful animal dressed up like a man. Silent and scowl-ing slightly now, he stared at her. This time when he spoke, he was elaborately polite.

"Why don't you, my dear," he said, "think about *not* going to Philadelphia this summer?"

"Why?" she asked, drawing back, at once in despair with herself for responding in the old way of suspicion and fear. "Why not?"

"Well, it's so hot, for one thing, and I know you to be a lady of delicate constitution."

Was he mocking her? Or not? Suspicions! Fears! Again! The immigrant, even after she has mastered the new language, blames ambiguity on her own mistranslations. If only I *really* knew the idiom, she thinks, goading her brain to work harder.

She ordered herself not to be suspicious. "Oh, no, I'm very healthy and can stand the heat fine," she said earnestly. "Once I worked in a laundry, there's no place hotter, and the foreman made me the pacesetter—"

Was he laughing at her or not? A kind of sneer crossed his face. Barnes was tired of his politeness. He was back to his scowl. "Not all difficulties are foreseeable." Was it a warning?

He left her abruptly, and she thought again of that bare room that was John's other side. Barnes was there too, filling the room with his dark power, his blunt speech, his passion to own and control, to crack whips, to drive wheels over anyone in the way. And now John, in her imagining, came into this room that was there on the other side of himself. He was looking for the warmth and joy he would feel when he found what he hoped would be in it. But there were two of them there, two passions, Anzia and Barnes. There was love and there was power, and they hated and were jealous of each other, though they both (even in her frightened fantasy she admitted this) loved John. Staring and staring into the bare room on John's other side as if the vision were real, Anzia saw John back out, back away, too much torment. . . .

It's Barnes's Philadelphia, she thought, shivering. I'll tell John I can't go.

7

Reclaiming the Body

John developed tension pains in his neck. "Hegelian dualism or New England repression—they all split mind from body, Anzia. I get it in the neck like this to prove to myself once and for all that thought and feeling are one. I know it in my bones now. Please, Anzia. Reconsider Philadelphia."

While she shook her head helplessly, no, John asked in a sympathetic voice, "Is it your sadness about your little daughter? But since your husband is not allowing you to see as much of her as you'd like anyway, do you think it would be so much worse in Philadelphia?"

She blushed, because she had not been thinking of Louise at that moment. Levitas—Arnold, her husband—was, after all, a good father. Anzia dreamed of bringing her child to live with her one day in a proper home, but she recognized that for now Levitas was a far better provider than she could be. When Louise was with her, Anzia lavished love and care on her. When they had to be apart that was another story, she could let other life flow in. John must be right, she thought—everything in life is tested by practical consequences. Pragmatism.

Having pleaded, John stood quietly. This was in part, she knew, because of strained neck muscles. All the same a powerful stillness came from him that surrounded her like an atmosphere. She wanted to comfort him—"Don't be unhappy, I'll go"—but fear of Philadelphia held her back.

One afternoon he told her that he had arranged to visit the studio of the well-known body aligner, F. M. Alexander. Barnes had already agreed to join them. For that matter, so had Harry Marsh, to whom John had also extended the invitation. He wanted very much, he said, to have Anzia come too. Alexander's ideas fitted in so well with his own that he thought Anzia would find the experience rewarding. Again she was uneasy; Barnes and Marsh would be there. Without having any idea what John meant—wasn't her head above her shoulders, her body above her feet?—she said, "I think I'm already aligned."

John agreed. "You're young, healthy. You spring from an expressive culture. But we can all benefit from F.M.'s methods."

Must Barnes go? she thought. She got up her courage and asked John the question she could never be rid of. "How can Al Barnes be your friend?"

John smiled at the question, as if he too appreciated its place in Anzia's mind.

"Al's moody but he's all right. Even if he were a bad lot, Anzia, couldn't I do more by staying his friend and influencing him?" After a minute, John said softly, "And if he were a saint, why would he want anything to do with me?"

She found his answer wonderful. Look, she thought, how John can take into himself a person so much his opposite! She felt, by comparison, narrow and dissatisfied. I am too much aligned with myself! John's answer made her burn, more than ever, with the fever for change. She was always challenging herself: Is that how you want to think? Is this what you want to be? Is this the self that's you yet?

"Barnes is a brilliant fellow," John said. "Not only in his work as chemist but also in his theories on art. You can learn from Al and Al from you. It's bound to happen."

And so Anzia found herself at Alexander's studio. In the waiting room, Harry Marsh rubbed at his right arm, which was sore. He was like some wounded animal that turned, now, puzzled and helpless, to nose at an injured limb. It didn't matter that she had often seen him lift that arm and shoulder in class and rub at it. She felt as guilty as if she had actually hit him with the flowerpot that day when she looked out of her fire-escape window and saw the black-hatted figure and suspected Marsh of spying.

"I'll bet," John joked, "it's because you've thrown too many punches at your enemies, Harry."

That made Anzia shudder. With an ashamed satisfaction she now pictured the flowerpot catching him on that arm.

John looked innocently eager. Barnes wore his usual somber frown and kept silent. Go to Philadelphia? she asked herself. Barnes's home ground? With Marsh there too?

At last Alexander's secretary brought them into the studio, done up in mustard and black. Small tables held bowls with two or three flowers. Chairs with carved wood backs and tapestry-covered seats were stiffly arranged at the center of the Turkish carpet. Barnes stood in heavy aloofness, and Marsh held himself in a kind of wrestler's stoop as if he might be attacked.

After another minute, Alexander himself entered the room with a bouncy stride, as if a special spring twanged in his foot. He wore a formal suit and sandals with thick white socks. Everything about him seemed freshly sprouted, like the white carnation in his buttonhole. He turned his sharp-featured face to address them.

"You hear my voice? The full production, the roundness, the depth? This is my true voice, a fine instrument. Once it was crippled. I opened my mouth and croaked like a crow. In the middle of a reading of my favorite recitation piece, 'Napoleon'—"

He interrupted himself to recite theatrically, " 'Oh, lonely exile! Oh, armored ambition pierced!' " Then he went on in his normal, slightly less theatrical tone. "In despair at the loss of my voice I devised my technique. Discovered movement in non-movement. The results—you hear my voice. Now you must listen and obey."

Alexander kept one arm raised while he spoke, like Maurice Schwartz in *King Lear*.

"We will not take ladies first. We will take the professor." He clapped his hands onto John's head, standing tiptoe to do it. "All your life your head has thought you. Now you must think your head. Think and direct it, forward and up!"

John's hands flopped at his side like fishes. In response to Alexander's pressure he folded himself into one of the chairs.

"Ah," said Alexander. "Terrible!"

He slid his hands down John's neck and back. "Now think, lengthen and widen!"

John lunged forward, seemed to topple upward from the chair.

Alexander folded him back into the tapestried seat. Unlike John, Alexander didn't feel obliged to think things through each time. He quoted liberally from himself. " 'Doing in nondoing.' 'Guarding against slipping back into bad old ways.' 'Reeducating the soul.' All this is in my book, *Man's Supreme Inheritance.*"

He patted John's neck and back. "We'll keep you here for a bit. So. In this manner."

With this springy walk he moved to one of the small tables and took from a drawer what looked like a brick covered with softening cloth. He placed it at the small of John's back, against the chair.

"If it feels dreadful," said Alexander, "remember you can't trust your feelings. You have felt wrong for a long time. You must come up with a new set of feelings which one day you can trust. I know these ideas will be clear to you, of all people."

"Wonderful," John said. "Truth in feeling at last."

Years of longing weighted his words. In a rush of feeling, Anzia decided, I'll go to Philadelphia. I want to. I must!

"Now." Alexander walked with energetic steps toward Barnes. "We take the gentleman from Philadelphia. Who acts and commands and collects." Alexander made a little springy bow. "With you I stress inhibition. To say no to yourself."

He stood on tiptoe and laid hands on Barnes's big head.

"You will direct your brain to say, 'No, Albert C. Barnes. No, you may not sit. No, Albert C. Barnes, captain of the ship of commerce, you may not have everything you want. And though you want to sit you will not sit."

Barnes's face grew red with the effort of attempting to say no to himself. His dark brows knotted.

"Forward and up!" Alexander's hands pressed down. Barnes landed in the chair with a thump.

"The war," Alexander said, "shows that what we call civilization is nothing of the sort. Like the nations we have moved from a savage state only to a superficially civilized one."

Anzia shuddered again. I won't go to Philadelphia. I can't!

She was still standing. By the time Alexander came toward her, Philadelphia confusion was making her sway like a tree in a storm. When his hands rested on her head he seemed to know what went on inside it.

"You also will experience difficulty in saying no to yourself, my dear Miss. Nevertheless! Think only forward and up! Lengthen and widen!"

Forward . . . lengthen—Anzia desperately wondered—what? A coattail of remembered dream—the angel and the scroll—flicked past. The chair edge touched under her buttocks, and for one moment she floated in a weightless crouch above the chair.

Alexander whirled around. "This woman's vertebrae have the ability to think!"

Oh, no, don't single me out, she prayed. Her body relinquished its anchor in the air and she sank, head awkwardly poked forward, into her seat.

John's body was fixed where it had been placed, and without moving his head he sent forth praise. "Good for you, Anzia!"

Neither Barnes nor Marsh granted her a glance. Alexander settled a cloth-covered brick at Barnes's back and did the same with Anzia and Marsh. Telling them to stay put, he left the room.

Marsh, in anticipation of his turn, began a rapid muttering. "It's all right if there's not much in your head to begin with. Then you don't have trouble saying no to what's there."

Barnes sat unmoving. "Stop that commotion," he said to Marsh from between clenched teeth.

John was slumped against his brick, thinking.

When Alexander returned, he looked them over. He gave a patting touch to John's head, slid his hand down his back, and adjusted the brick.

"Never mind if it still feels odd."

"I welcome every newness." John's voice was humble. "Whatever announces something happening in feeling at last."

My love, thought Anzia, I'll go with you.

Alexander went to work on Harry Marsh. The massaging touches continued all along his neck and back—"Lengthen! Widen! No, you will not stand! Forward! Up!"—while the master of alignment drew Marsh's heavy body willessly up from the chair.

Marsh had certainly been drawn to a standing position. A large bump distended the front of his gray trousers. His body began to shudder. His jaw dropped open; he gasped; his face drained of color. In an instant his trouser front was soaked.

Anzia looked away and prayed not to be seen seeing. Her mind was made up. I'll stay far from any city he's in!

John was leaning forward to think and noticed nothing. His brick thumped to the floor at the same moment that Marsh thudded into his chair with a timber-cracking sound.

"Well, I must go, F.M.," said John.

"But Mr. Marsh"—Alexander was severe—"must stay on for an extra session. And Dr. Barnes might benefit from that as well."

Barnes laid his clasped hands in his lap and glared at his assistant with a mixture of disgust and rage.

In the street John said cheerfully, "Poor Al. It's me, not him or Harry, that's the worst pupil Alexander ever had. It's a wonder *I* don't get kept in after school."

His face was flushed with excitement. His hair and clothes looked wind-whipped, as if instead of sitting quietly in one of Alexander's chairs he had come from the open cockpit of an airplane.

"I was on the wrong foot all these years. You're the one who got my spirit's feet straight, Anzia. Bless you!"

She reached up to smooth his hair, stroke the back of his rumpled jacket to the shape of his long elegant spine, and press the gaping pockets to his slender hips. Once, she knew, he had been a shy, self-conscious, feeling-tormented young man. Then without transition or mercy he'd clapped himself into the iron armor of abstractedness, disembodiedness. He had separated himself from the world of passion and poetry by a moat full of sharp-toothed mind.

Now when she saw the warm light spark up in his eyes, a flush of color pump into his cheeks, her ambition was to make them stay. She felt like a polar explorer shielding a flame from extinction in wind and snow.

Alexander had suggested that John remove his glasses and use his eyes unaided. Anzia guided him past obstacles and made sure he was not run down in the road.

"Try to think of us this summer, Anzia, in Philadelphia. Working, living, side by side. . . ." John turned to her with a loving, half-blind gaze. "What a joy to be near you and watch you continue to grow."

She bowed her head and allowed him to slip over her brow the garland of growth. She wished there were spikes in it so that she could pierce and kill the dybbuk of the lower depths that screamed within: *Where are you going with him? What can you be to him?*

"In New York I'm in my own place," she said in a low voice. Lower still, she murmured to herself, "Alice is your wife."

"Yes, you're in your own hard-won place, which you've made for yourself," he answered with sympathy. Then, almost with clairvoyance, John added, "Would you want to be Alice? Do her endless obligations to others add up to a life you'd want?"

She thought of warning him not to misunderstand her that way, not to imagine that being cut from responsibilities was her happiness.

"I think often of the injustice to Alice," John said softly.

Anzia was ready to admit her part in it. But that was not what John meant.

"Alice had a mind as lively as anyone's. When she became the rock the family relies on, she gave up her connection to the Alice she once was. You're not Alice. Your whole life is dedicated to the wisdom of becoming Anzia." After a silence his words came painfully. "You don't answer. Does that mean there's a chance you might not go?"

When she stayed quiet he stopped in the middle of the street.

"I meant it to be a paradise for us, Anzia."

She made what was truth for herself a joke for John—"That means there'll be a serpent"—and heard his relieved laugh as they walked on.

If I do go, she vowed, I won't be so easily fooled by the snake into swallowing an apple the way Eve was. The plain fact is—Anzia was figuring it quietly to herself—if Eve had grown up on the Lower East Side like me, she'd have known better than to be sold a bill of goods by a fruit peddler without even a pushcart.

Posters warned against "loose lips." The old ghetto superstition haunted Anzia: the evil eye keeps jealous watch of every moment of happiness.

One evening she tried again to see her little daughter. Levitas barred her way at the door.

"If you want to comfort your child," he said, "stay a night."

"Don't make her pity herself," Anzia begged. "Children understand these things. Don't prevent me from seeing Louise and showing how much I love her. Let me tell her again that we'll be separated only for a little while. Let me see that she's happy."

"Then don't run off when darkness falls."

"I can't live with you. Why make me say it again?"

"Anzia, for God's sake," he burst out, "have some pity on *me!*" Then he collected himself. Fumbled at his vest buttons, needing to close them. "Only for her. I won't take what's begrudged me."

From somewhere down the darkening street Anzia felt herself stared at by a figure lurking in the gloom of evening. She pictured a bowler hat, a florid face. The fecal smell of cigar smoke drifted back. Was it Barnes's assistant or her own fears trailing her?

In the morning her throat felt swollen, as if she'd been swallowing down tears all night in her sleep. Her head felt hot, too. She walked back to her old neighborhood to see Elkish. Not a doctor or a druggist, he had the reputation of a man who could for a small fee in his kitchen match a medicine to a malady.

"Open. Ah."

Elkish had shaved off his beard with his piety: a man, after all, in a scientific profession. But his dirty fingers still longed to squeeze and stroke. Sometimes where the beard had been, sometimes her own arm. The odor of herring and onions leaped from his throat to hers as he breathed.

"Oy-oy-oy. Pus. Red with yellow."

He withdrew from a drawer a wad of cotton from which he brushed a few bread crumbs and fastened it to the end of a pointed stick. This he jammed into a bottle of brown liquid, then brought it dripping to her opened lips.

"Stay!" he commanded, as she flinched from the smell and the burning touch of it. "You're gonna jump around?" Elkish irritably threw the stick onto the wooden kitchen table. "Goodbye!"

But he had no intention of letting her go, and addressed scornful prophecies to an invisible listener.

"Pus she got on her tonsils, very nice! My own daughter I'd take and grab her by the neck and push it down and that's all. This woman got time to be sick and lay in the hospital? Good luck to her! Next comes dipateria." Elkish translated names of diseases into his own notion of the familiar. "Kholerya. Flitzentza."

Anzia saw herself fevered and delirious in the jammed wards at Bellevue, unable to let John know where she was. In desperation she opened her mouth. Elkish plunged the stick once more into the brown bottle and then down her throat. At once she gagged deeply. "God, how it burns! Who could invent such horrible stuff?"

"You and I should only have one percent of the profit on such horrible stuff." Elkish's smile was pitying. "What that man makes in a week!"

"Who makes?"

"What is it, you live on the moon? Wait!"

He lifted the bottle to let her read the label: *Fortieth and Filbert Streets. Philadelphia.*

When Elkish repeated the name of the city, respect embellished it. "Feelahealthier! Not New York! Where every crook spits in a bottle and calls it medicine! Feelawealthier!"

He hammered the top back on the bottle with his buttocky palm. "You thought it was maybe Chaim Yankel's mixture? You never heard from Barnes, the Argyrol king? The Feelageltier millionaire? The *owner* from Feelageltier?"

Anzia felt as if someone had gripped strong hands around her neck. She stuck a finger down her throat and began to gag. "I . . . must . . . get him . . . out!"

The kitchen healer pushed at her. "Out yourself! Crazy woman! Don't come back!"

In the street in front of Elkish's tenement she vomited into the gutter, ridding herself as much as she could of the mixture concocted by Albert C. Barnes, the owner of Philadelphia.

. . .

Anzia was always slipping into bookstores, searching for John's books, looking for periodicals that had his name in the contents. She opened the pages and read for as long as she dared, without making the store owners aware that she was a customer who never bought. She saw John's mind reasoning, reasoning, adding another qualification, teetering on one foot, catching its balance, teetering on the other. This is good, but of course if it goes too far in this direction, it is not good, then some of the other is a corrective. Impulse is necessary to change things, but thought is important to evaluate it, and habit is bad when unchecked, but essential also for giving shape to things. . . . Oh, it went on and on! But what do I do to *live?* she silently screamed at the pages. At least Elkish, who grabbed you and stuck a swab down your throat, gave a remedy that sometimes worked. He didn't stick one end down your throat and then the other end too, to try to cancel out the first. But now—she thought— maybe she also was suffering from the German Mind, wanting to have answers given to her instead of learning to creep along the ground with her ear down, listening to life like a doctor with his head on a patient's chest.

She had to burst out—out!—of the bookstore and walk rapidly along the streets, sniffing the smells around her and looking at all the sights. These over here she loved, those over there she hated, and she knew it in a minute, and that was what it meant to be alive! Still—once you're alive, then what? Is this what life is for you? she demanded. A bazaar? Sniffing, looking, liking, hating, laughing, crying, and scribbling it down, that's all?

She slowed her walk. You know very well you go too far in one direction, she told herself. And she turned her steps back, creeping like a snail, to the bookstore, where she would swallow down some more of the two-ended stick of John's pragmatic thoughts.

John's daydreams welled up. Of the greatest sweetness. The most awful sentimentality too, John supposed. But great, great, satisfying sweetness, warm, enfolding, a hint from the deep of what was so absent in solid life that the deep's longing sent up an apparition of it in veils and smoke.

It happened, this time, on his walk, working out in his head some sentences for an essay on the value of pragmatism in the classroom, ensuring for children the practical application of every scrap of information they receive. Reading a play by Shakespeare in which war is enacted they will naturally wonder about the meaning of war and peace in their own time, leading to interviewing family members who served their country and, going further down the field, to questions about peaceful warfare they observe in aid of certain causes—suffragettes, for one, waging war on their opposers—and then watching a demonstration for which they might feel moved to create posters and placards, leading then to questions of design and visibility, color, form, optics, crowd psychology, aural phenomena, experiments back in the classroom with pitches of voice and audibility, projections of tone and their connection to body alignment (Alexander's theories), relationship of actor to audience and so by way of the round world back to Shakespeare—and all self-engendered!

After this flow of ideas, John stopped and closed his eyes for a moment. Another theme altogether abducted him. He saw himself dressed in antique garb, a pilgrim toiling with a staff along a dusty road, coming upon a young woman scantily clad, bruised, her clothing royal but ragged as if she had fled from pursuers, lying in an exhausted faint in the dust. Lifting her, he felt the beat of angelic wings at his back; a sort of glory heat ruffled the hair on his head. Like Elijah he was taken up to heaven, but unlike Elijah he pressed against his belly a half-clad female, legs and arms twined about him in gratitude.

Such daydreams, vivid and detailed, flashed up complete and disappeared in seconds, unlike the formless weave of thoughts, cogitations, analytic explorations that absorbed him for hours. How to put the two worlds together inside one man? There was no waking way. Except the poems. Love poems. God poems, too! From an atheist and a rationalist! What if the poems were all daydream? And what if the jarring embarrassment that came upon him after awakening from one of those dream trips of his—canoeing on a cloud, was how he thought of it—was what he ought to feel about the poems too? An I-am-not-myself embarrassment, like the old woman in the folk tale whose dog barked at her one day. In humility he ought to expose these dream trips as well as his poems to Anzia. His last hope of wholeness.

As he walked, his spirit sometimes soared straight up on a song line of poem, sometimes puffed out its feathers in the torpor of heated daydream; sometimes it dropped cold and dead, shot down by his own stare of astonishment. He stooped and shambled, forgetting Alexander's alignment principles. His mind struggled and stretched and reached, forward and up and sideways, to catch a rein on its own runaway horses. "Oh, God, allow this little departure from my accustomed self," he prayed, atheist-rationalist that he was, "and permit me to hurt nobody by it. A suffocating philosopher does no one any good."

8

A Trip to Paris

In the end the forces of Philadelphia were too much for Anzia. The President of the United States himself took an interest in John's Philadelphia project, though by roundabout means. First, President Wilson proposed that John travel as Wilson's emissary to Europe. This was only one of many missions that John undertook throughout his life. In 1937 he would travel to Mexico as head of an American delegation to hear Leon Trotsky defend himself against Moscow Trial charges that he had betrayed the Russian Revolution, begun in the same year that John and Anzia became lovers. John concluded that the charges were a frame-up. Trotsky, he believed, had not betrayed anything. A few years earlier he believed that the Revolution had not betrayed anything either, and was full of idealistic hopes for it.

By the thirties Anzia's success as a writer was dimmed (*Bread Givers, Hungry Hearts—forgotten!*) by America's plunge into the Depression. She read about John in the newspapers with the sense of unreality we feel about former lovers who make their way in the world without us. Had John betrayed his own revolution? She could not read the word "frame-up" without seeing Philadelphia and Impressionist paintings and their own two selves framed in the heated, loving nights.

An ends-justifies-the-means revolution is perhaps the last thing of which John Dewey, with his commitment to the goal of gradual buildup of growth and change, ought to have approved. The democratic, humanistic mind is sometimes capable of looking at its opposite political number, which seeks "temporary" obliteration of free will in totalitarianism, and of feeling not the expected revulsion but an admiring fascination. All this may add an onion layer to what John and Anzia were up against by the simple act of falling in love. Though when we consider what quicksands underlie those homely words, "Opposites attract," "simple" ought to be struck from the vocabulary. Between John and Anzia was a whole world of difference to allure them and promise healing. But first they had to take a sea voyage.

In May of 1918, Woodrow Wilson asked John to visit Premier Clemenceau of France and plead Wilson's plan for a penalty-free peace when the war was won. "I am ready to go without food, sleep, and anything else that supports this poor material body of mine," President Wilson wrote to John in his usual martyr-mimicking tones, "for the sake of a great Christian goal: making peace while waging war. Are you willing to sail on a troopship to France and see what your fine philosophical mind can accomplish?"

In spite of Alexander, John's neck was giving him extra kicks. He took to holding his head even more to one side than before, even though Alexander warned that this would let loose a new chain of bad reactions. Anzia thought that the way John held his head gave him the look of always considering some problem.

"I'm not inclined to get on a troopship," John said. "It's not the torpedoes and submarines. I feel so dammed up sometimes, I'd welcome the possibility of explosion. I'm just skeptical about Wilson's utopian ideas. He's personally popular, all right. But if you ask me it's just as well his peace programs are laughed at. There's a trait in Americans that can be annoying, but sometimes it saves their souls. They lift a hero up in their arms and let all his ideas fall away like bedclothes from a baby."

John went to Washington to meet with the President, who wished to discuss with him the guidelines for the mission to France. John in his turn decided to set before President Wilson a sketch of the valuable goals and purposes involved in his own proposal: a study of Polish immigrants now living in Philadelphia. Polish reluctance to embrace Americanization could provide what John so desperately sought: a place where he and Anzia could embrace all summer long.

Although the meeting had gone well, John came back disappointed in the President of the United States. Wilson, a short-legged man with a big head, had stood against the window in his Washington office, his large jutting ears catching the light so that it shone through the outer cartilage, reddening it to match the stripes in the American flag beside the presidential desk. The familiar presidential pince-nez had gleamed coldly at John as the President lied about his background, claiming roots in the American Revolution. John knew Wilson's mother and paternal grandparents had been immigrants.

"What a damn fool thing for him to do. He missed the boat on what the real aristocracy of this country is, the real red-blood royalty. When you come down to it, there's not much red blood in his war politics, either.

" 'We have no selfish ends to serve!' " John quoted Wilson's words, spoken when the United States entered the war. " 'We desire no conquest, no dominion. We seek no indemnities for ourselves, no material compensation for the sacrifices we shall freely make.'

"There's no pragmatism in it," John complained to Anzia. "It's all saintliness and martyrdom. It reminds me of my mother." His clear eyes clouded. "I'm not keen on carrying that message to Clemenceau. The terms of peace, when it comes, will have to be worked out by give-and-take. Wilson wants to impose Utopia."

One day John announced he'd suddenly realized what could be gained if he said yes to President Wilson's offer to send him to France. He and Anzia could go together. "You'd be the diarist of the trip! You'd be the ship's secretary. My God, Anzia, we could be together on that whole voyage and then in Paris!"

"Go across the ocean to be together?" asked Anzia. "Is that the reason?"

John said there were other considerations. "Peace, and the lives of our boys, and making the world safe for democracy, to use Wilson's windy words. I'm thinking of those too."

Anzia was thinking that of all the passengers on the boat

that had brought her to America, she was one of the few lucky ones who wasn't seasick the whole time. That terrible trip had not made her eager for ocean voyages. Still—Paris!

This was between student examinations and the start of summer vacation. Anzia wondered aloud how John would explain the trip to Alice. John looked into the distance. "Alice knows there's a war on," he said softly.

John even saw a way to include Alexander, who could conduct alignment sessions for the soldiers. This made the voyage seem less intimate, John explained, than if just the two of them went alone with those thousands of troops. There was gain in it for the country as well, John said, giving Anzia this example of the logrolling pragmatism that lies deep in the American grain. She was grateful that he hadn't suggested that Barnes and his bodyguard come too, in order to offer the American doughboy this model of wealth and privilege to aspire to.

In wartime, the simplest things are impossible. The most impossible things are sometimes easy. President Wilson personally arranged for their passage on the *Leviathan*. It was a captured German vessel now carrying American boys to the trenches of France, and it had the fastest turnaround time of any ship—twenty-six days to the French port of Brest and back. Wilson sent a message that he was getting down on his knees to pray for a torpedo-free trip.

The ship was crammed with men. They slept in shifts, to make best use of the berths. The sea air relieved the tension in John's neck, even though his mission was so urgent. He planned to visit Clemenceau in Paris and discuss from a philosopher's point of view Wilson's victoryless peace over which there was so much Allied alarm.

The days passed quickly. The troops were cheerful young men, confident of victory. Neither John nor Anzia was seasick. They watched maneuvers and "abandon ship" drills and alignment lessons by Alexander. Men volunteered for instruction after Alexander explained that proper posture could speed up a man's response to shell fire by 100 percent.

During the late watch, in that balmy springtime air, John and Anzia found warm nests for their blanket. They projected meanings in the darkness for all the new boat words: "berth," "life preserver," "hold," "transport." When darkness fell they often berthed inside a well-provisioned lifeboat, snug with equipment and gently rocking, under the great cannons themselves. As John pressed his burning face to hers, Anzia imagined it was even possible they might detonate a charge over the dark and dangerous sea.

"We'll find some little hotel beside the Seine," John said, "and just lie there in each other's arms." He believed the icy winter that New England and his evangelist mother had laid on his soul would once and for all dissolve in Paris.

Albert Barnes had talked to John about the painter Gauguin, who lived in the exotic heat of a South Sea island among beautiful native women. "Naked," Barnes said, "except for their flowers." Barnes told John about the Impressionists, Van Gogh, the hot colors of Arles, the heated summer picnics of the French countryside, the nudes of Renoir. "Their flesh is made of roses, John. I give you my word you'll see them all in Philadelphia." John said to himself that he had already seen such loveliness in Anzia's little room.

In her mind Anzia painted John and herself into a rose-colored bedroom. Its curtains blew back from a window overlooking the Mediterranean blue of the Paris sky. She was the woman who lay on the tapestried couch. Already she felt the soft tones stroke themselves onto her breasts and hips, enriching them.

The ship docked in the dead of night. In darkness and silence they rode along bumpy back roads and at dawn Anzia was astonished to hear a language that sounded foreign but not French.

"What are they speaking?" she asked John.

"British."

"In Paris?"

"It's a catastrophe of the war, Anzia. We're not in Paris. We're not even in France. Mines were laid off the harbor at Brest, and the captain was ordered to take his ship elsewhere. He docked us in Southampton. We're in London now." John sent a cipher wire to Wilson, to say he would try his luck with Lloyd George. Wilson wired back his intention of getting down on his knees to pray for John's success.

"I wish Wilson would leave off mentioning his knees and God in the same breath," John complained. "I believe in God, all right, in my own way, but I never for a minute think I can get Him to do anything but His own will. Look at us ending up in London."

Like God's ear, Lloyd George was busy elsewhere. The consul offered to introduce John instead to an important British intellectual and pamphlet writer. The man's wife was also a writer, though the American consul said he had "damned little time, with all these dispatches, to do any lady-novelist reading" and couldn't give John any clues in that direction. The safest thing when introduced, the consul suggested, was to say, "I hear your plots are humdingers!"

Alexander went to visit relations in the South End. John and Anzia were taken to a house in the Richmond section of London.

"A visit to a pair of British writers is a cut above a prime minister," John said.

"Look, the name of the street." Anzia pointed as they stepped from the car. "Paradise Road." A plaque beside the bell read HOGARTH HOUSE.

John spent the evening out at a meeting with their host, the pamphlet writer, a lanky, bony, long-nosed man with a typical English look and a typical English politeness.

"My wife is not at her best," he said, "and is confined to bed. I am always optimistic that she may feel better in the morning."

Anzia was assigned a cot in the dining room, which was cleared of furniture except for a small printing press and a table covered with flat wooden boxes, all having to do, she supposed, with the pamphlet writer's work.

Black draperies curtained the windows to keep even a gleam of light from showing. During the night Anzia heard noises of someone wandering around in the dark of the room. Her first thought was that John, who had been given a bed somewhere upstairs, was searching for her. A match was struck, a candle was lit, and a tall figure slowly emerged from the darkness. It was a woman. Her long hair hung over the shoulders of her nightgown and down her back in great disorder. Anzia saw that she was as skinny as a skeleton. She carried the candle to a table next to the hand press and, with long bony fingers, picked letters of type from the font rows in a large wooden box. Now and then she shook the box, making a faint hollow rattle.

"Are you the writer?" Anzia had gotten out of bed in great excitement.

The tall woman shook her head violently. "I am the wronger!"

"I'm a writer myself, so I ask," Anzia said. The woman was silent, and Anzia tried again. "I see you work at night. I did the same when I was at the factory. I came home at night and wrote and wrote." Still no answer. The house was damp and chilly, and both of them were shivering.

"It's a good idea to print your own writing the way I see you're doing," Anzia said encouragingly. "When I get back to America I'll try it. Abraham Cahan of the *Jewish Daily Forward* won't touch my work."

The woman tilted her long bony body backward. "Jews," she said. "My husband. His mother. But Greek is what the birds sing."

"Is he really?" Anzia was too struck by what she heard about the husband to bother about the birds. "That's funny. He doesn't sound Jewish. I suppose he had a terrible struggle to make himself into an Englishman. My struggle is to make myself into an American. And he"—she pointed toward the upper stories of the house, meaning John—"struggles to make himself into something else too."

The writer's lips moved, but no sound came out. Her deep eyes stared. They looked hungry.

"Would you like something to eat?" Anzia asked, as if the woman were not in her own house.

"I don't eat."

"Or have a nice hot drink? Mrs. . . . ?" Anzia had not caught the names of the hosts, though readers by now will have recognized the clues. The shivering writer was the aristocratic Virginia Stephen Woolf, in one of her periodic bouts of anguish and madness, and her bony husband was a man who had come from the opposite end of the earth to meet and marry her, the Jew up from Putney, Leonard Woolf, who became her nurse and who had hit upon the idea of the printing press at Hogarth House to give sane employment to her nonwriting hours. She shook her head. Her bony hands trembled over the tray of letters. As if she picked the name from the box she said, "I'm only Virginia."

"Please," said Anzia. "Go up to bed now. Your husband will take you in his warm arms. He's not too polite for that, I hope."

The hostess shrank away again, in that slow backward leaning. Her eyes deepened and filled with tears.

God in heaven! Anzia whispered. Into her own arms she folded the shaking figure, who bent down like some long-necked creature in a zoo and rested her head on Anzia's shoulder.

It seemed her husband did not keep the mattress warm. Anzia herself slid into Virginia's freezing bed, where they clasped one another like the Brontë sisters on a cold night at the vicarage. There were sounds from below. Someone was bumping furniture in the dark.

"Leonard is printing," Virginia said.

"It might be John," said Anzia, "trying to lie down in my cot. In a minute he'll discover I'm not there." Anzia was right. There was another series of bumpings before the house was quiet.

In the morning, John was discontented but Leonard was elated. Virginia, John and Anzia learned before returning to the ship, was better.

"Paris probably wouldn't have worked anyway," John said philosophically on the return voyage. "I don't speak the language. They might have put me together with Alexander. Or Alexander with you. Or, Paris being Paris, all three of us together in one bed under a canopy as big as a circus tent."

From New York, John sent a wire to Wilson describing the temper of the English as sane and humanely civilized. He cited his long talk with the British pamphlet writer, a typical Englishman, John said, who rejected every form of punitive peace treaty.

Wilson wired back: FULLY ENDORSE YOUR PHILADELPHIA PROJECT. YOUR SUMMER'S INFORMATION-GATHERING WILL BE A TURNING POINT FOR AMERICA'S PEACE EFFORT.

Anzia was not sure why. It would take the cynical interpretation of Irving Bitman, one of the Philadelphia researchers, to explain it to her weeks later. For now she understood that the federal government had had a hand in bringing it about: somehow or other she would be going to Philadelphia after all.

John bought bagfuls of fruit from the pushcarts of the Lower

East Side and brought them to Anzia's room. Undressed, they lay on her bed and fed each other, letting the juice run down and stain their skins with what John said were French colors. Their bodies became sticky with fruit and love serums.

"We'll go back to our beginnings." John licked up a little pond of nectar from her navel, then moved downward. "Make ourselves over . . . the Adam and Eve we want to be . . ."— he was having difficulty with breath and words—"Philadelphia . . . our Garden of Eden . . . our Paris."

Anzia was finished with fighting Philadelphia and gave back licks and kisses. Love, as everyone knows, can bestow on innocent Eden more wildness than the wickedness of Paris.

"Here's a coincidence," John said after a while. "That house Barnes has taken for the project is on a street called Richmond. That's the name of the section in London where Hogarth House was located, you remember. I call that a good sign."

Anzia was glad to hear it.

"And the name of that street in London," John reminded her, "was Paradise Road."

Anzia made up a joke for John. "A Philadelphia serpent meets a Lower East Side woman in the Garden of Eden. 'You want learning?' he asks. 'Me?' she answers. 'I burn for it.' 'So eat. Knowledge of good and evil will be inside you like Abel and Cain.' 'I can't swallow such concepts,' the woman says. 'I don't touch a thing that's not pragmatic.' The serpent wears out his little stubby legs looking for a Pragapple tree in Paradise, and nobody hears from him again."

John laughed and Anzia forgot Barnes. Maybe she didn't really forget. But she told herself that now she was a philosophical pragmatist like John, things weren't only black or white. By this time she was helping John color in pictures of the paradise John told her Philadelphia would have to be.

By this time what else could she do?

PHILADELPHIA

Peach-Skinned Nudes

Merion, a Main Line suburb, was in 1918 a place of large es-
tates, leafy summer shade, and aristocratic country silence, all
within an hour of Philadelphia.

In Albert Barnes's home in Merion, on a hot June night,
dinner is done up in grand style. The long table in Barnes's dining room is set with fine linens and silver. Young Negro women
serve in spotless starched uniforms. Huge fans at the open windows bring in sweet smells from the gardens and blow them
around the guests stiffly seated there. A few professors from
the University of Pennsylvania are keeping strict watch over
their words. Some business tycoons with culture-craving mates
are struggling to keep their voices down, as they've been warned
by their wives to do. Conversation limps on, unencouraged by
their host, who frequently turns his heavy face away from the
guests and toward John, to see if he will join the conversation.

John is staring with fascination at the pictures on the din-
ing-room walls, where swift, brilliant, light-dashed men and
women are eating, drinking, leaning on a hand to listen. They
mirror pastimes at this table. But how much realer, how much
more full of life! A starched frill scratches at his cheek as a
crisply uniformed servant leans at his side and from a silver dish

spoons him out a roasted potato. What's realer than a potato? He stares without seeing, pokes a fork without eating, compares his dark, confining jacket to what men and women in the paintings wear: a few dots, some lines, a brilliant lump of color. The paint is thick, rich.

A woman enters the room and sits down. She fits herself into a space between John and the next guest and smiles into his eyes. She unbuttons her blouse, exposing her breasts. She is realer to him than the women in the paintings, who seem realer than this life. Her thigh presses hot against his hip under the table's lace. John's imagination has summoned Anzia in a fantasy as firm as her flesh.

Debate springs up: public education in Philadelphia. The guests attempt to draw John out.

"A far cry from your goals, Dr. Dewey."

"I'd rather not comment." His hand gives a startled no-no wave. "On schools I haven't seen." (Old Dissembler, he comments to himself on that, with an inward flush of shame.) He's not at the table, at least not in the form they think, keeping up with the conversations they hear: Germany's atrocities, Wilson's peace plan. They give him credit for being deep thought-sunk. But he's gone from them; he's upstairs on the bed where he and Anzia are pressed together, two more nudes in a house that's full of them.

Late that night while everyone sleeps, he rises from his bed and returns to the paintings. He tries to summon up some of the concepts Al has talked to him about. Shapes, forms, balances of architectural structures in the canvases. You can't approach a painting by its subject alone, or confuse subject with substance—that's never what the artist did in the first place, no, myriad impressions, ideas, responses, sucked in by the intensity, the passion. . . .

Mid-carpet he stops. After a moment, his meditation continues: to approach a painting without consideration of subject altogether is again a one-sided affair, a splitting of flesh from concept, and the poorer for it.

He has been slowly moving toward the canvases hung on the wall facing him. Now he stops again. He is wearing a somewhat tattered purple-tinted bathrobe, once blue, whose tasseled belt trails on the floor behind him like a mangy tail, having worked its way free of its first loop and being within moments of escaping the second. Alice had bought him a very nice new robe and encouraged him to wear it, especially when traveling. But since he has forbidden her to throw this one away—it is only when he is wearing his oldest clothes that he feels able to push off some of the weight and pressure of the world—he is most often likely to put his hand to the old bathrobe, especially if Alice is away.

He puts his hand to it at this very moment, sliding it again and again against his hip before he realizes that the sides of the comfortable, worn pocket his hand is blindly seeking have detached themselves from the fabric and that nothing but a flap of material, out-turned and emptied like a palm, hangs where the pocket ought to be.

Never approach anything at all for its literal content only, which is all too quickly emptied out. Never approach a painting for subject alone. The thought repeats itself as he approaches the canvases. Soon he is staring once more at the naked figures bending, lying, leaning. "Odalisques," Barnes calls them. Some fondle beads that dangle between bare breasts. Others lie with open palms against naked thighs.

I am not myself, he thinks, light-headed and swaying. So much the better.

The surfaces of those paintings, when you get up close, are broken by brush strokes. Art's miracle, like love, makes the beholder see things whole. In one of those lying-down women he sees Anzia. She leans on her side and one braceleted arm, a hip thrust forward, breasts half in, half out of some gauzy scarf, the nipples relaxed, salmon pink.

He is drawn irresistibly to the canvas. He lowers his lips to it, to those warm spots of womanly pink, and kisses back and forth. . . .

"Jack! I thought—I had no idea it was you!" A dark-wine dressing gown of silk is belted over the broad body, and from it Barnes extends powerful arms to throttle intruders. "Of course, Jack, examine the canvases all you like."

John's breath has broken. He turns to the pictures to hide it.

"I'm delighted," Barnes said. "Notice the remarkable color masses."

John is afraid his harsh, straining breaths will be heard in

81

the silence of the room, but happily a great noise overwhelms them, coming from the upper reaches of the house. In a minute Harry Marsh, his florid face puffy from sleep, comes pounding down the stairs, belated belligerence in every stroke of his slippered feet onto the Oriental rug.

His bathrobe is a pugilist's terry, with its hood half risen, like a cobra's, over the back of his head. The tie of the robe has not been done up. His pajamas are yellow, with a green diamond pattern. Seeing Barnes and Dewey there before him, he fumbles in astonishment with various closings at his front.

"I heard—!" he blurts out as he bursts in. "There was—!"

Barnes doesn't bother to turn around. "Get to bed, you idiot!" he snaps.

The next day he gives John a session with the paintings. Tree-lined landscapes, greens turned purple under sunrays pumped from the artist's thumbs, flower gardens like riots or revolutions, chairs, tables, flower vases jumping around on the canvases like spring lambs. Peach-skinned nudes. Velvet-skinned nudes. Naked women who look as if the artist's semen (John won't say a word about this to Al) sprang out and coated them with the pearl-shine of the stuff.

"Rhythmic relations of the greens," Barnes says. "Comes around the edge here and leads the eye to the center." He lays a thick finger on the navel of a nude.

The sessions go on through the afternoon and begin again after dinner. Barnes is a man possessed by the works he possesses, obsessed by his own paintings, and—yes, John can see it's true—passionate about art. But enough is enough. Before Barnes can reach the end of one more row of paintings, John is pulling a schedule from his pocket ("I'm deeply grateful to you for the art lesson, Al") and looking up trains to Philadelphia. Barnes, after a startled moment, rises handsomely to the occasion and offers John the use of his car and chauffeur for the drive from leafy Merion. He sees John off, waving from the doorway like an anxious relative.

The house Barnes rented for the researchers in the Polishtown section of Philadelphia is a place of small dark rooms among the connected rows of houses, two-story, flat-roofed, with a single step before the door. In the parlor are a sofa and chair upholstered by a hard hand into convex surfaces closer to a slide than a seat, a few dark-shaded lamps, and an oval rug of brutal braid that crunches underfoot.

Barnes knows degrees of comfort and keeps the students to the nethermost notch. Those rooms were the first hint to Anzia, after she and the three other researchers arrived in Polishtown, that she had not been far from the mark when she imagined how Barnes would fit them into Philadelphia. To John the choice of housing suggests a fascinating aspect of Barnes's mind—the eccentricity that can sometimes translate to creativity and power.

Anzia is always a little shy of John after an absence. Now that he has traveled late at night to be with her here, she searches his face to see if the stay at Merion has harmed him. Meanwhile he studies hers.

"Don't," she begs. "There's nothing good to see."

But he stares hungrily at the broad cheeks, the eyes planted full on the surface above them, not recessed like most, and Orientally elongated by the down-slanted folds on the upper lids. Above them the eyebrows are center-peaked, in symmetry with the upper lip of her full, expressive mouth. It is a high-planed face that looks Slavically impassive till she speaks, then is all motion, every pore and surface heated. He remembers—he always remembers it, a kind of spiritual anniversary—that miraculous moment in his office when he caught her in his arms. Even soaking wet, her body radiated more heat than any woman he had ever held.

She is shaking her head as if to blur her features. She believes, touchingly, that they bear fingerprints of old faults she longs to change.

Because of a different kind of heat—heavy, oppressive— they don't fully embrace in her room but walk instead to the nearby bank of the Delaware River, to a secluded bit of it Anzia has found. There they place themselves, lying on her spread-out shawl, within the brilliant night. Millions of star points stick in the sky. The moon has exploded, or Barnes's French pointillist painter has done it.

John speaks in the whisper of someone who stares up at stars. "Al showed me his treasures. His paintings, his famous naked beauties. Anzia—they don't hold a candle to you!"

River sounds sing in their ears. The stars whirl and vibrate, heating them on the grass like suns. He clasps her with a sigh strong enough to blow out all the lights above, then uncovers her breasts.

"Lovelier than any Frenchman's pictures. Grander than Gauguin. Better, oh, Anzia, than Paris!"

He has the feeling of floating through endless stretches of sky. In the cool darkness of the riverbank, moonlight silvers them. If they don't dare be wholly naked for fear someone might approach (no one so far does), they are daring enough. The part of himself that John bares seems to him like some silvery fish leaping powerfully up in moonlight. The same light illumines Anzia's beauty. Happiness encloses them like a golden frame.

John breathes into her ear. "And the paintings—the paintings, Anzia, all around Barnes's dinner table! Thank God, Philadelphia is what we hoped it would be!"

In the joy of the moment, she does not remind him that she has not been shown the paintings or dined at Barnes's table.

10

Philadelphia Is Paradise

Luxury was everywhere in Barnes's great house in Merion and nowhere in the Philadelphia house he rented on Richmond Street for the members of the Polishtown Project. The place was small, stuffy, and empty of everything that gave comfort. Anzia's room here was as spartan as the one in New York—bed, dresser, desk, chair.

A few days after they had moved into the house, Ellen Wright knocked at Anzia's door. She was tall, innocent, eager, the daughter of a geography professor.

"It's exciting to live this way, isn't it?" she said. "Just like the natives of Polishtown!"

"Yes," Anzia answered. In spite of herself, she added dryly, "You'll remember how much fun it was especially when you've gone back to your family's comfortable apartment in Manhattan." Though Anzia longed to enlarge her judgments to resemble John's all-embracing ones, by now her cup of confusion was running over, and that is never a good omen for the generous impulse.

Ellen Wright continued with undiminished eagerness anyway. "Albert Barnes's plan is right here. All we have to do is

85

follow it." She had brought along pages of ideas from Barnes about how to climb up inside the head of a Pole.

"I'm to visit schools the Polish children attend and see how well they do with teaching the English language and American customs. Irving and Emmet will talk to men in the factories and taverns and mingle there. What language do the men speak among themselves? Do they read only Polish newspapers? That's what they'll look for. But first we consult these texts and memoranda Barnes has given us for uniformity of approach." Ellen's neat fingers tapped each point on the page.

"Is my name there?" Anzia asked, suddenly apprehensive. She would not have been surprised if Barnes had brought her there to leave her out again.

Ellen traced a line beneath Anzia's name. The sight of it, even her married one, made her breathe easier. "Mrs. Levitas looks at family life, possible translator." But then there was the note next to that: "In important cases, services of Polish residents who speak English are preferred."

With one hand he gives, with the other takes away! "Why should we stay indoors," Anzia asked bitterly, "and only read the books and papers Barnes sends us about what the project ought to be? Why can't we use our own ideas too? Does he think we're all tubes of paint and he can squeeze out what he wants?"

There was an elegant grace to the poise of Ellen's neat, dark-haired head, but for a second it wobbled with surprise. "Al Barnes is our sponsor here. I don't understand"—her voice trembled a bit—"the point of arguing with him over every little thing."

"Sponsor doesn't mean sweatshop boss! If we have our own experience we should use it. Haven't you learned that from the seminar?"

A frightened look gathered in Ellen Wright's eyes. Anzia recognized an old self, fighting hard for fear of being crushed before anything even started. Is this what you call change? she rebuked herself in disgust. What is growing in you besides hair and fingernails?

She apologized to Ellen. "There's nothing for you to worry about. You told me what I'm supposed to do. So now I know it, and if I don't it's not your fault."

· · ·

On July Fourth, patriotic displays exploded in the streets. Flags, bunting, parades, soapbox orators, victrolas playing marches. Anzia's fellow students stayed indoors, obedient, poring over pamphlets and questionnaires. Anzia moved around the celebrating city, among the posters she knew from New York. UNCLE SAM WANTS YOU! COLUMBIA CALLS. SPIES ARE EVERYWHERE.

Irving Bitman and Emmet Trumbull, she realized, would knock their heads against walls in the factories and taverns. The Poles in Philadelphia wouldn't want to talk to strangers. Barnes had said the Poles were "a cyst on America." The project researchers were supposed to examine the cyst, analyze it, prick it open. Meanwhile the Poles would go on. Anzia knew how immigrants found ways to outwit their tormentors.

Barnes's Argyrol factory, a big square building with blue lettering at the top, powerfully occupied the corner of Fortieth and Filbert streets. Anzia watched the straining horses pull away wagons loaded with crates of the mixture. She could still taste it at the base of her throat, bitter as Barnes himself.

The city was melting in the heat; the tar of the road sank under her shoes. John had been called away again. Anzia waited for his return with a longing that breathed with the steam of summer.

Because John and Anzia were reckless, her house companions were cautious. There was no sign of them in corridors or common rooms when John was there. But they know about us, Anzia thought, as each in turn came to see her while John was away.

Emmet Trumbull knocked at Anzia's door. His excuse was to request some translation from a Polish newspaper. Soon he was asking her a forthright question.

"For God's sake, Anzia, tell me, what makes one person fall in love with another?" Emmet was stocky, fair-skinned, and mild, with a broad smooth-lipped mouth like the mouths of certain fish and with flat blue eyes, now shadowed. Love torment appeared to strike at him unfairly, as if nature had formed him for friendly encounters only.

"Ellen has all the lightness of spirit, goodness, and depth of being I lack."

Anzia was astonished that he could make such a mistake.

"I seem to have none of the qualities Ellen wants." Emmet went on with his love complaint.

"Why not? You're kind," Anzia said. "You have a warm nature. Show a little more of yourself, don't be so reserved. Shine a little more like the sun so she'll want to unwrap herself in your heat."

"I don't feel like the sun," said Emmet. "I feel like a rainy day."

"The truth is, a person has to need to fall in love." Anzia wondered why she said that. Hadn't she herself fought against love till it swept over her almost without her knowing?

"Of course. We know that change can't be imposed on anyone," Emmet agreed gloomily. "God knows if we're followers of Professor Dewey we have to believe that. A person has to need and want to change."

The brightness in Emmet's broad face dimmed. His stocky body shrank before her eyes. My own success in love is making me careless with poor Emmet, she thought.

"Listen, Emmet!" She thought it was better to scold him than to let him sink. "Who's to say that need won't suddenly come?"

When Ellen wanted to see Anzia she knocked elaborately, little repeated nervous knocks, not loud but persistent, like a chattering hand. Her neat, dark, nervous head almost tremored in its anxiety to look and not look. Anzia kept her door narrowed when answering, even if John was not there. It was good practice for when he was.

"I don't know," Ellen said, "if I can do my assignment. I never know what people are saying. They prefer to look blank rather than use what little English they possess to answer questions. Even the children understand I'm on a hopeless mission. As I left the schoolyard, I felt some light objects strike my back, some between the shoulder blades, some lower down. I didn't turn around. Al Barnes will be furious with me. I have so little to report."

"Don't worry about him," Anzia said. "You did your best. But if you like, tomorrow I'll come with you and translate."

•   •   •

Irving Bitman knocked, then spoke to Anzia in a quick, bitter voice after he came into her room.

"Probably I will be unable to obtain an appointment in the philosophy department at Columbia even though I might be the best student in it. The country calls itself a democracy but moves on wheels of money and family connection. Where does a Jew come in?"

"Look at me, look at you," Anzia said. "Immigrants or immigrants' children. But we're here, allowed to join the project."

"Allowed to join!" Bitman himself looked bitten. He was small and dark and moved his hands jerkily when he spoke, as if he intended to use them less.

"Children of immigrants can become rich and famous. Look at Barnes," Anzia said.

"They never enter the inner circles of power. Even Barnes. That's one of the reasons he's got it in for everybody."

"Who wants to be there? You go your own way in freedom, what more do you need?" Anzia was fighting against Bitman's gloom, a thing it was easy to catch.

"What is our whole project about? Americanization. What is that? We say we believe in pluralism. John has certainly written against the melting-pot idea. But aren't we trying to find out why the Poles don't give up their Polish customs and language faster? If Poles in Philadelphia, why not Jews in New York? Don't people say the same about them? Yes, people say, give us diversity of background, richness. But if we're really different they don't like us. They may seem to for a while," he said darkly, "but in the end they go to their own kind."

What is he driving at? Anzia asked herself. Some terrible ending for John and me? Even if he didn't mean that, she would resist agreeing with Bitman. He had already decided on his attitude, already enacted his rejection. She could not accept it. What she needed to believe now was that every hurdle could be jumped. *Make every moment a mountaintop. . . .* But did that mean there were no barriers, only botched efforts? Should every failure in America be blamed on the one who fails?

A host of faces from the ghetto swam up before her. Gentle types guaranteed to go under, who couldn't scramble to grab opportunities. Yes, but the others who kept on—what if doors kept shutting in their faces too? The notion came back, demanding attention. What about John's idea of how we affect our fate? Did that mean Bitman himself, with his bickering brilliance and distrust, would be responsible for his own rejection if it came? If it came would that be because he had prepared the way for it?

She did not like to follow the course of Bitman's argument. Surely John could not have intended his optimistic beliefs to mean that those who could not climb to success in America had only themselves to blame. If that was true, then at the bottom of so many hopeful, generous words, at the underpinning of so much exalting thought, there might be something bitterly cruel.

She wished Bitman would go. Suddenly he switched subjects. "Does Ellen Wright ever say anything to you about me?"

"Ellen Wright? About you?"

Bitman stood in Anzia's doorway looking unhappy. "I suppose not."

"All right," said Anzia, understanding at last the meaning of Bitman's bitterness. "Tomorrow I will mention you to Ellen and tell you what she says."

This whole house, she thought, is heated by love.

Years later, Anzia tried to tackle in her writing the tricky question of why someone like Emmet Trumbull could not achieve his desired union with Ellen Wright. Why not—since he had cast them as opposites (she was everything, he was nothing)? The truth, Anzia saw, was that Emmet and Ellen were as alike as twins, each innocent and trusting and trying to fetch up flamboyance elsewhere.

Bitman's irritable brilliance attracted Ellen. On one of those long, dull Philadelphia evenings she confided to Anzia—and then, regretting it, withdrew even further from her—that her mother had suffered from her father's lack of brilliance (though it is difficult, she explained loyally, to be brilliant in geography). But the attraction of opposites did not do its work with Irving and Ellen. Irving's oppositeness was also what frightened Ellen off. No one should oversimplify such matters, Anzia thought. There is mystery in them.

In Philadelphia, John came and went. Often, to their disappointment, and despite what John had hoped, he was forced to meet family obligations in New York and Long Island. What stayed in Anzia's room was a present from him, a shiny black Underwood typewriter like his own. Sometimes he made use of it himself, working on his memorandum to President Wilson. "Confidential Report on Conditions among the Poles in the United States," he called it. On the slow, crashing keys he worked out an analysis of the two Polish factions of the exiled government. The one he favored for its democratic views was headed by a man called Kulakowski. The other, led by the great pianist Paderewski, John considered autocratic. John wrote that the purpose of their seminar was to "ascertain forces and conditions which operate against the development of a free and democratic life among the members of this group."

John suspected that one source of trouble was the attachment of the Poles to the Papacy. He thought the Poles were already planning their return to Poland after the war—a loss to America's work force.

A little pile of notes for a story had accumulated on Anzia's chair. She pressed herself against John's back, bent over the machine, and kissed his neck.

"When we're like this I see you were right," she said. "Philadelphia is paradise."

Hard as it would be to get away, John promised they would visit another paradise, Atlantic City. He pictured stars at night above the ocean, themselves below on heated sand, love overspilling their riverbank and running on to the great sea.

At last, the researchers were invited to Merion. Barnes's car gleamed at the curb on Richmond Street. The four of them ran to it past the knives of neighbors' eyes.

Silence during the ride. Spies are everywhere, including in the chauffeur's seat. Loose lips sink ships. Anzia kept her hopes to herself, that John would surprise her in Merion.

They rode to another world. Green acres, huge trees, and, behind them, when the car stopped to let them out, a house of rough gray stones with a red tile roof and a huge oak door. The cave of a wolf, Anzia thought. Then at once of course she told herself to open her own spirit's oak door, to stop this obsession with who and what Barnes was, to show John her new understanding. In case he was there in Barnes's house.

Barnes stood in the hall with a cigar in his mouth, his hands stuck in his pants pockets. He was scowling, as if he resented ahead of time the hours they'd consume, the food they'd eat. He named them to his wife, Laura. She was a delicate blond woman who wore a pale blue gown and seemed to stand without breathing. Marsh, the bodyguard secretary, on the other hand, seemed to breathe without standing, so poised on his toes was he, ready to detonate himself in discharge of his duty, an arsenal for art's sake.

Then there was a hugeness of chambers. Carved wood overhead and rich carpeting beneath, its depths dragging at their feet. Faint with hunger for delicacies, they passed by a sideboard with crystal decanters that gleamed red with wine, and plates that bore finely rotted loaves of white cheese, blue-veined and green-marbled. As if these sights were not brilliant enough, they were led on to where a blaze of colors—blues, reds, pinks, and whites with the shine of wet pearl—leaped from the walls. Faces, figures, gardens, parks, seasides. Families, children in sailor suits and white dresses, sashes, hoops—all composed not from paint but from light.

"Oh, oh! The beauty!" the graduate students said. But they looked aghast. These faces and forms on canvas were broken by jagged strokes, then stitched together with seams of light like whitened scars at the places of growth and change.

Anzia made up her mind to show Barnes she could hold herself together in the face of art as well as he could. She swallowed hard and kept quiet. The pictures were crowded together, the frames jostling one another like a Hester Street mob.

Barnes thrust his hands deep into his pockets and surveyed the richness. "I saw in Paris how to shove pictures up against the walls." Mysteriously, he added, "At Gertrude Stein's." He glanced at his group of listeners, raised a thick eyebrow in boredom as he realized no one understood what he was talking about, and abruptly turned his back.

After that, Barnes seemed to abandon them. They followed Barnes's wife, who followed him. More rooms. More paintings. Barnes's dark house was full of lit-up, just-born beings whose skin gleamed like treasure in a cave.

Suddenly Barnes was addressing them again, pronouncing the names of these new artists with possessive pride: Gauguin. Van Gogh. Cézanne. Renoir. Matisse. He said them over to make sure they got them right. At the same time he glared accusingly, as if he knew they wouldn't.

Anzia repeated the names of painters and paintings. Gauguin, she whispered to herself. Cézanne. Renoir. I'll know them by the time John comes back.

She sat in her room in Polishtown, writing a story about a young woman who returns, educated, to her Lower East Side family and is shamed by their immigrant ways. Parents and daughter end weeping in misery. But Anzia does not weep. Like Chekhov, like Tolstoy, like the Impressionist artists who would never cry all over their work. The prose boils: "God in Heaven!" cries the daughter in the story. "Such dirt, such noise!" "Ay-ay-ay!" weeps the mother. "For this I had to have a daughter!" "Leave out," writes Anzia to herself in the margins, "exclamation points!"

Still, ink spattered onto the page at the ends of sentences. Stroke-point! Stroke-point! She despaired of improving her style, but also was secretly, strangely proud. No amount of willing away could dislodge her true voice.

"Trust it," said John. "It tells the story of your generation as only you can. On those exclamation points your voice is borne aloft like majesty on a litter, anointed in the deepest recess of your being." John's speaking voice sounded wistful as it contemplated the sureness of Anzia's writing one.

11 ···≼

A Lion of Art

Anzia memorized painters' names for John, letting Frenchmen drop from her lips, when he returned, like the crumbs of crisp baguettes.

One night in her room, too intent on love to saunter to the riverbank, John suddenly pulled away from Anzia as if unconscious of his own movements. He clutched his arms, jackknifed at the hips, and pitched forward toward a chair, his forehead nearly on his knees.

Oh, God, I was right, Anzia thought; sixty isn't thirty!

"Should I run into the hall?" she asked in fright. "Should I yell for help?"

John stayed motionless for another moment without answering. Then he scared her a second time. He sprang from the chair to the typing machine and began pounding something out like a man desperate to record his last testament. She watched the words hammer onto the page, letter by slow letter:

The sting of your kisses
Swells my lips,
Changing the shapes of words
They utter

"Next time"—she was in tears—"if I think it's a heart attack and it turns out to be a poem, tell me. Please!" She rested in his arms, recovering. "I worry about you more than I knew I did."

Now that the poem had passed from him to paper, he was lightened and relieved. "Don't worry about me. Just tell me if you like it."

She wondered if he was speaking of their lovemaking. Or was he asking about Philadelphia?

"I like everything we do together," she said.

"God knows I do as well. I meant the new poem."

"You know I love all your poems."

"I know you're generous to me in everything. But I mean for itself as a poem. I gave you"—it was a reproach—"honest criticism of your cooking class."

The cooking class meant nothing to me, she silently protested.

"The new poem is wonderful," she said. "For itself it's wonderful, and up and down and all around itself it's wonderful." God is my witness that I'm not lying, she thought. If only God can understand the way I mean this. "All the poems are wonderful, and it's wonderful that they're here." They'll get better, she told herself. What he needs now is encouragement.

"Yes, that is wonderful, wonderful! I'm grateful. Do I need to say it, Anzia?—the dry stick I would have been if you hadn't found me? But I need somehow to know more now. Which one is more realized than another? What direction is best?"

Her fright returned, as if this was some fresh sickness. "Don't look with critical eyes at what's newborn," she pleaded. "Say a blessing instead."

Tears had come to his eyes. "You always feel, instinctively, the right thing," he said. "I have so much to learn from you!"

After that, he placed new poems on her bed nearly every night.

"It's growing, this little heap."

She greeted the poems with her lips on the pages.

One evening she showed him some dark wool she had bought to stitch his poems together into a little book.

"Don't do that now, Anzia." He added quietly, "I'm thinking of giving them to someone to read. Someone I trust."

"Who is the someone?" Her heart began at once to thump itself to pieces, as if the attack she feared for him was happening in her.

"A friend and colleague, Morris Kaplan of City University."

"But what is he like? Who is Morris Kaplan that you want to show your poems to him?"

John was patient as always with her ignorance. "Kaplan is one of our great critics of art. With one of those large brain-crammed heads you sometimes see on such men—a fierceness of concentration and dedication. Mention art to Kaplan, and he becomes a lion." She could see John enjoyed the image. "His mane of gray hair stands up, his broad flat nose sniffs the air."

Despite herself, Anzia reached out both hands to cover the poems. "Aren't they just ours?"

An expression of pain came into John's eyes. Anzia quickly took her hands away. She regretted the gesture. Wouldn't her protectiveness of the poems look to John like lack of faith in them? For all the optimism of John's philosophy, she sensed pessimism below the surface. She wondered if he had always been like this or only now, because of the war, or because of Alice, or because—who knew why? She thought again about what she had already asked herself: When they met might he have been close to something like nervous breakdown? He was happier now. Poetry no longer lay buried and choking him. Still, she wondered if now he was even closer to nervous breakdown because his happiness at their being together, and his poems, all increased his consciousness of everything else in his life that made him miserable. Those feelings he once said he kept pushed beneath his protective armor were now rising and clamoring for attention. Why am I harping so much on breakdown, she asked herself, when everything we do is building up?

"Dearest," she said, "don't mind my old ghetto fearfulness."

"Are you afraid I'll find out they're no good?" The furrow between his brows sharpened, like pain being cut deeper. "Is that what you're afraid of, Anzia?"

"How could they be no good?" she answered, pleading. "Everything is in them."

"What harm, then? Are you afraid we might be revealed? I would never consent to publishing."

Does that mean, Anzia asked herself, *he* is afraid we'll be revealed?

After a while she found other words. "I'm afraid for your belief in them. So near the beginning, anything can be crushed."

John's debating mood suddenly fell away from him.

"How you lavish concern on what concerns me," he said, tender-voiced, brushing the long fingers of his hands against her cheeks.

She would gladly have lavished more, but he was doing now what she had so often seen him do with others. He looked away, lost in thought, and that was how the conversation ended. He was always telling her that her intuitive wisdom was deeper than his learned wisdom, but his resolve seemed to develop from some aspect of himself she never touched. His ability to pour out work—papers, lectures, essays, articles for popular magazines like *The New Republic* and *Seven Arts*, as well as for scholarly academic journals, plus preparation for new books forming in his mind—never diminished, no matter what.

She remembered how John had once quoted to her from an essay by William James, the philosopher whose writing style he so much admired. James had compared thought to a white feather quill that pierces at one end and arches back gracefully to brush the mind at the other.

"How I'd like to summon such images to my writing." John had sighed.

"Oh, you can, you will," she'd promised him.

Now the poems were here. But it was too soon to uncover them to strangers' eyes.

12 ···✑

Circular Questions

Sometimes Anzia thought she had won John over, convinced him that his poems should be allowed to develop in safety, far from Morris Kaplan's lion jaws. Didn't John know better than anyone that it was process, not result, that mattered most? Wasn't that the heart of John's educational philosophy? At other times she worried that John might still consider submitting the lamb (his poems) to Kaplan (the lion). If it was anybody else's poems, Anzia thought, John would have more pity.

She decided against asking him outright what he planned, for fear of stirring up the very impulse she hoped might be subsiding. Her anxiety boiled within her and had to be taken for endless walks along the Philadelphia streets.

One day she joined a small street crowd. A patriotic celebration, she thought, till she saw they were taunting a young woman trying to hand out circulars. She was neatly dressed in a navy suit, her skirt boot length like Anzia's, her hat brim filled with artificial flowers, every one of them trembling.

"Friends! Sisters!" she cried.

Men and women in the crowd screamed at her. "Sin against God!" "Replacements for the poor lads we're losing over there!"

"Doesn't know there's a war on!" "Wants the Bolshies to take over!"

"The poor," the woman cried back. "Disease! Tuberculosis! Misery! How can a sick woman care for fifteen children?" Her voice was too wavery for this street work.

One savage in the crowd yelled, "Drag her home by the hair!" The rest joined in. "Shame!" "Indecent!" "Did you leave your babies for this?" "She ain't got any, a mother couldn't say such things!" "Shut her up!" "Get her out!"

Anzia felt someone had put a match to her blood. In her loudest voice she shouted, "I am a mother!" and rushed to the soapbox. They would kill you, she thought, if they knew what kind of mother you are, and what you've done with your own child.

John's dream of progress filled her mouth. She took a deep breath, prepared to share the whole thing.

"First," she called out to them, "you must develop your own selves as much as you can! Then it will be time to create other beings who—"

Her cheek was slapped hard by something unseen. Her companion on the soapbox screamed, and the air was filled with what looked like angry birds flying at them. They struck and broke open, spattering filth. There were shouts and screams, and then sirens. Anzia snatched at the woman's hand and ran with her from the crowd.

"Tell me your name," she gasped as they ran.

"Barbara Westerfield. I must catch my breath!"

In the safety of an alleyway Anzia learned that Barbara Westerfield's family had threatened to disown her because of this rough street work. Still she persisted, frightened as she was.

"When what they ought to do is take you in their arms." Anzia did it for them, rocking Barbara against her filthy shirt-waist for minutes while she sobbed out her fear.

Finally Barbara lifted her head. "The clinic isn't far," she said with a brisk, sensible air. "We can clean ourselves there."

They started in its direction, but as they approached they heard a new uproar, new sirens and shouts. When they arrived at the place, knots of women stood in the street among police vans and fire trucks.

"They've attacked us here too," Barbara Westerfield said. Then the despair left her voice. "But she's standing there among the women. She'll know what to do!"

She led Anzia to a slight, pretty woman speaking calmly amid the shouting crowd. Anzia was introduced as a benefactor who had saved her from a mob.

"And this," she said proudly to Anzia, "is Mrs. Sanger."

In a soft and even voice, as if talking of everyday matters instead of blood, prison, and death, the reformer Margaret Sanger, after nodding to Anzia, went on with what she had been saying to the women gathered around her.

"Among the poor, men collect children the way millionaires collect art treasures, to make known their power. Whoever interferes with that feels the weight of their rage. If we recognize that element alone, we will understand what happened here today."

As if Margaret Sanger knew Barnes, Anzia thought. "I can bring your message to the women of Polishtown," she said, letting excitement carry her away.

"Can you? Remember, there are those who will do everything they can to stop you," Margaret Sanger warned.

Anzia said it was nothing new, the world was full of people trying to stop her. As matter-of-factly as she could she added that she expected to visit the birth-control clinic herself, now that she knew it was there.

"It's all a ruin inside," Mrs. Sanger said. "Chemicals that irritate the eyes thrown everywhere. No one will be able to enter the place before end of summer."

Too late for me, thought Anzia.

Soon after, Anzia walked along the two-story row houses and picked one where she could see many small children on the other side of a ground-floor window. The kitchen table was piled with sewing, a laundry vat boiled on the stove alongside a pan filled with frying sausage. Heat and grease smells never affected her before, but Anzia felt suddenly sickened when a woman, her belly big, opened the door.

Anzia began with questions about the woman's daily routine. Soon other questions flew from Anzia's lips. Questions from Margaret Sanger's circular, and circular questions anyway, when you thought about them. "Do you want more children? If not, why do you have them?"

At first the woman was too shocked to speak. She assured Anzia the priest and her husband said anything else meant sin. Then her husband himself, waiting to go on late shift at the factory, came in from the next room to see. He had taken his suspenders down and they flapped around his knees like an apron, a symbol of the domesticity he suspected Anzia had come to interrupt.

Anzia was ready with her speech. The President of the United States had endorsed the project with which she was connected. It was under the direction of a famous professor from a great university in New York. They had an office in a nearby street, in a house like their own.

"Sure, we know." Drops of sweat flew wildly as he shook his head. Unwilling to share Polish, he addressed her in broken English. "Men and women in one house, we know! What you do there? We know!" His fear, like a boiling vat, shot out scalding drops. "Now you come here. Ask all questions. You all go jail!" His arm reached out to pull his wife protectively to his side.

He followed up with a stream of oaths in Polish that Anzia understood all too well. Suddenly, she felt they had all made a terrible mistake in not announcing themselves to this community. Polishtown had them stamped as spies, and immoral ones at that.

A meeting was in progress when Anzia got back to the house on Richmond Street. Barnes was there, handing out more questionnaires. She saw John sitting quietly in a corner and felt such a spurt of joy that her knees trembled. Reckless with happiness, she blurted in a loud voice that she had talked with the Piruszkis a few streets away and learned more than any questionnaire could tell.

Barnes sat immovable, then muttered darkly that the best of plans could be spoiled by upstarts.

John won a quiet compromise, to cut short the number of meetings and start in Polishtown next day, no sense any longer in putting it off. Anzia was to be more "scientific" and gather more evidence before coming to conclusions. Anzia agreed because John asked it.

She was miserable again when John was invited to Barnes's house in the evening. The residents of Richmond Street boiled their potatoes and fried their sausage. Their stomachs were supposed to learn what the stomachs of Polishtown were lined with.

"My God," Ellen said, "a diet like this!" She vowed to get to some of the better grocery stores in Philadelphia. Lovely fruit aspic. Lovely salads. Lovely loving looks she got from poor Emmet, whose digestion, already ruined by love, soured his breath.

No one spoke to Anzia. They blamed her for bringing out Barnes's wrath. She volunteered her turn at the cooking and nudged sausage pieces over in the pan. It wasn't hard to understand an immigrant woman's life if you had a cooking spoon in your hand and disapproval all around you.

"I worry about you," John said. "Are you comfortable? Happy?"

Anzia traced her fingertip along his brow, smoothing it. He had slipped away from Barnes's house. "Don't worry about me at all," she said. "I have never been happier."

When he was gone, she walked through the Philadelphia streets again, looking at the foreheads of the men who passed. All of them seemed darkened by imperfection. In her mind's eye she saw the clear, broad brow, the gentle brown eyes, the rumpled clothing to which John was entirely indifferent.

In their early days together, dazzled by John, she had called that love and thought of the attraction of their opposite selves as if they were linked in some chemistry experiment. All that seemed long ago. She was almost afraid, now, of the way her stomach clenched and burned when he came into the room. "This," she whispered into the stifling summer air. "What is the meaning of this?"

Along the river a fat cloud shaped like a bear rearing up was suddenly tinged with pink, then it melted down to a small golden hassock that narrowed itself and spread out into a running snake. Anzia walked past a huge old willow that grew on the bank. It leaned far over the edge, not just branches and leaves but the thick gnarled trunk too, all its bumps and outgrowths stretching that way as if every particle longed for water. Picturesque. But she was sorry to see it—an old tree that had soaked up seasons, with no sense of how to live its life or manage its great longing for the river. One day soon it would over-balance itself altogether and yank itself up, as if its trunk were a lever and its ball of roots no more than a nail in the ground. It would drown in what it most desired.

13 ···≺

"My Verses Grow from Your Body"

John brought more pages of poetry to Anzia's room. She lay in his arms and murmured them over.

"You've opened my heart, and these things pour out now"—his eyes so vulnerable she moved her body as if to shield the poems from harm—"I hope they're not just all gush."

"Could I be so happy to read them if they were?" You, Kaplan, she murmured in her mind, Never put your lion's head near these poor unguarded verses. She pictured the poems lying on the snowy ground like a wounded deer under Kaplan's slavering jaws.

The pages had fastened to her naked skin like paper to the printer's plate. John peeled off sheets of words. "As if," he said, full of wonder, "my verses grew from your body."

It was then she felt Kaplan's teeth sink into her moist hip.

One evening of heavy rain, when the streaming streets smelled of sulfur, John gathered his poems from her room.

"'Yes, all right." Anzia saw he had made his decision. He would carry the bundle to New York, to Morris Kaplan, the lion of literature.

•   •   •

When John returned to Philadelphia, he climbed the stairs to her room. Though he had published essays and articles and volumes filled with ideas on philosophy and education, this time was different. Poems were personal, poems exposed you, and Kaplan's eyes were the first critical eyes to see them (Anzia's eyes didn't count; Anzia's were loving). Like any author of soul-baring lines, he was already, at the very beginning of the wait for Kaplan's words, exhausted and depressed.

He removed his clothing and lay on Anzia's bed. For once she had gone out without her shawl, leaving it on a hook behind the door. He covered himself with it, closed his eyes, and waited. After a while, in the curtain-darkened heat and peace of the room, he fell into a deep sleep.

He half woke when someone knocked, but slipped easily back. Through sleep-hazed eyes he thought he saw the figure of a woman. She carried a large pack of papers, which she lowered onto the top of the bureau.

He lifted an arm from the bed to hail her. The woman turned, startled. Eager, he raised himself onto an elbow, while the shawl slipped from his bare chest. The woman brought both hands to her breasts and clutched them.

"Oh-h-h!" She pronounced it with a moaning sound, as if from depths of love. She slid from the room, while he slid back to the dream on his pillow.

By the time Anzia returned, the account of John's visit to Kaplan had mingled with the visit of the woman to the room while he slept.

"I experienced something like a hallucination. A strange figure came and went. Was it a touch of madness in me? She was like the woman you encountered at Hogarth House." He gave a saddened laugh. "Or it might have been the muse, flitting away."

"What happened in Kaplan's office?"

" 'Manuscript of a friend,' I told him. I was protecting my hidden self again, Anzia. My old affliction. I told my friend Kaplan that lie. 'Needs expert opinion,' I said. 'Wider response.' "

"You were right to say it. What did he tell you about your poems?"

"He read them, is all I can say. Glanced, really—very quickly, from first to last lines, up, down, flicked with his eyes. A wart on his left eyelid kept disappearing."

"That was his excitement! 'The lines burn in the hand. The phrases leap from the page.' Did he say that?"

"Those are your words, Anzia. Do you think they would come again from the mouth of the art critic, is that what you mean?"

"Why not? Why not?" She wanted to run to the art critic and stuff his mouth with her words right this minute.

"In fact he was silent. Though after a second or so he turned that grand head of his toward me and repeated, very thoughtfully, what I'd told him. 'A friend's poems,' he said. 'I'll reread them carefully.' "

"That shows he respects them! You see?"

"Then he asked me about Barnes and why he doesn't answer his mail."

"What does the U.S. mail have to do with your poems?"

"I suppose it means Kaplan must have some grievance there. It seems he hasn't been able to get in to see Al's pictures. I told him Al's besieged by petitioners, and that it's not easy for him to separate the sincere from the time-wasters. I told him to get in touch with Barnes again, and that I'd certainly put in my two cents with Al for whatever it's worth. Kaplan said he'd take my word for it that Barnes wasn't leaning on his bit of power. He said that when he came to Merion next time he'd bring my poems along, in case Barnes tried to bar him at the door."

Too uneasy to hear any more about Kaplan or Barnes, Anzia crept under the shawl's openwork weave to join John. As they caressed one another through the net, love and sanity alike seemed a matter of reaching in through gaps. But she could not stop thinking about Morris Kaplan. In her mind he was always there, always sniffing with his lion's nose at a handful of newborn love poems lying, still moist, on the ground. And John, in her mind, was running for his life toward poetry and love, pursued by lions.

Just before she fell asleep she realized who the strange woman in her room must have been. It was Ellen Wright, of course, who must hate her for breaking all the rules.

14

Money with No Smell to It

Marsh took Anzia out for a drive in Barnes's open touring car. This must be John's doing, she thought; he must have asked this favor of Barnes. She wished they could all have saved themselves the trouble, and her the strain, of riding with Marsh in Barnes's car. But having been asked, she could not refuse. Marsh sat stiff and forbidding, aping his employer. Anzia sat at the edge of the upholstered seat in the back with Marsh, the silent chauffeur up front. She looked at the bright brass door handle on her side and imagined how it would be to jump out into the road.

They drove down beautiful Main Line streets with big trees in even rows and sparkling white mansions behind the trees. Marsh began his tour talk, so bitter it burned like Barnes's mixture in her throat.

"Old Philadelphia. Old houses, old porches, old families, old boot-scrapers, old ass-wipers! Stingiest meanest people in the world, think their snot should be in museums. If people knew how Philadelphia treated Dr. Barnes!"

She asked what Philadelphia owed Al Barnes with his fine house, his art collection, his good business, his wealth. Marsh gave her a furious look.

"You know what new money is?"

"What you didn't have before and you thank God you have it now."

"Don't talk like a fool! Money can't have any smell to it. It has to be drying out in the sun so long you can pretend it's crumbled into something fine."

"But now he's turned the new money into paintings that all of Philadelphia wants to see."

"They can see his backside, as far as we're both concerned." Marsh, like his master, ground his cigar in his teeth. "You know what Philadelphia thinks of people from the Neck? We're garbage to them." He gave her a grimly challenging look. The bridge of his nose had been battered until it was as broad as its base; his cheeks and chin were hillocked with lumps. "Just let anybody come near to criticize! He's a genius. I don't sell Professor Dewey short, but all he does is sit and think. Dr. Barnes does everything—art, science, business, *and* philosophy. How can you compare?"

You can't, Anzia thought. "In America," she answered, calling on newfound worldliness, "garbage can be perfumed if it gets an education and on top of that makes a million dollars."

"He sweated blood to get where he is." Marsh was biting his cigar to pieces.

"So now he's there."

"Oh, no, not all of him. Part of him is still back there, a dirty-nose kid so smart they had to let him have a charity-chance at school. I'm so lucky," Marsh said. His voice thickened and grew muffled with emotion. "I don't know why he picked me out of the slums. But I'm not just a bouncer or a bodyguard. I help him"—his look defied her to laugh—"catalog his art." He waited, and Anzia kept absolutely still. He went on, nodding his head for emphasis. "When Dr. Barnes trusts a person, he educates them. The world doesn't know that or give him credit for it either. But they will when he gets all his books written. He's just as much of an educator as Professor Dewey!"

Anzia said only—using considerable restraint—that she knew what he meant when he talked about charity; she had also suffered from the insults of charity ladies.

The comparison infuriated him. "They were nothing to Dr. Barnes! He despises their dear old University of Pennsylvania with its mummified science and art departments. He rose far above them. He studied in Europe. He went in for chemistry the way roosters go in for cockfighting. Kill or be killed."

Too bad for anybody, Anzia thought, who doesn't know the difference between himself and a chicken.

Through the car window there suddenly came into view the tall spire, flying an American flag, of Independence Hall. Marsh nodded in its direction.

"Declaration of Independence," Marsh said grimly. So much talk of rising above had seemed to lower his mood. "All you immigrants dream of grabbing a look at the documents."

"Can we stop?" In her excitement, Anzia forgot that she meant not to show excitement. "Can we see?"

"What would you want to see for?" sneered Marsh. "You think one of your ancestors might have signed it?"

If not mine, she thought, then not yours either.

That was the finish of conversation between them. They spent the rest of the automobile tour in silence. When it was over Anzia wondered which of them was more relieved.

She thought of what Marsh had said about Barnes, though, when she went on her own to North Broad and Cherry to see the Pennsylvania Academy of the Fine Arts. Built to look like a Venetian palace, it was filled with dark, stiff portraits by Thomas Sully and Gilbert Stuart: *George Washington. Lord Landsdowne*. West's *Death on the Pale Horse*, Peale's *Francis Scott Key*. She thought of Barnes coming here as a boy and feeling shut out of all that dark dignity. Afterward she went by trolley and then walking some of the way to see if there really was a place called the Neck. She found it below something else named Kaighn's Point, stuck on a needle of marshland at the meeting of the Delaware and Schuylkill rivers.

As a wind brought the stink of fertilizer and bone-boiling plants to her nose, it was clear that anyone born there could find his way back blindfolded. She felt as if stinging grains from the nearby Pennsylvania Salt Company Works had been flung into her eyes. Impossible to picture Barnes as a little boy, but she saw *some* child trapped in the foulness, gazing up with despair.

"Across the marshes, the City Hall tower rearing up with its statue of William Penn." She had to tell someone about the

Neck, and she picked Emmet. "A boy growing up there would notice that every day. It might mock him or inspire him or drive him crazy with a desire to get out and up on that tower himself!"

"Growing up in a falling-down shack and looking at ugliness every day," Emmet agreed with a sigh. He was deep in love with a woman who didn't care for him, and in the pain of it he pitied the whole world along with himself. The dark glow of the parlor lamps shone gloomily. "Poverty, marsh rats, drunken brawling men, women going mean, boys going bad. I suppose in his own way he's a great man. I suppose," Emmet added after a pause filled up with another sigh, "that an out-and-out strong man like Barnes must be a relief to John in a way. Someone who bullies people as a matter of course, just punches straight out and doesn't worry about delicate matters of human response. Although," Emmet added, "Barnes can be so correct when it suits him that it's excruciating."

Yes, excruciating, Anzia thought. She wished John had picked someone else for a friend. She wished Barnes lived in Kansas. I wish, Anzia wished, against all the higher laws of pragmatism, utilitarianism, and *How We Think and Learn* by Professor John Dewey, that we had gone to Borneo.

15

Renoirs and Peignoirs

Barnes brought the researchers back to his treasures again. He didn't mind sending out an invitation to the four student starvelings, Bitman, Trumbull, Ellen Wright, and Anzia, as long as John wasn't there. Once, after they arrived, he said a word to his wife. She left the painting-crowded room for a minute and returned, leading two men in work overalls and dirt-caked boots. Their black skin gleamed under the bright oil-painting lights illuminating the canvases. Barnes had selected them from among the men who worked on his place. He was giving them the benefit of his special instruction, trying out his theories of education (they were mostly John's) in art.

"All right, boys." Barnes set them before a painting in the deep-carpeted salon, to exhibit what they had learned from his teaching. "Tell us about this beauty." He pointed his finger at a picture by Renoir—mother and nursing child. *Maternity*.

The big hands of the men, creased with heavy labor, hung at their sides.

"Go on, Junius," Barnes urged. "Come on, Lem."

"Rose tones," said Junius shyly. He was a tall, slender, handsome man of about twenty-five, with the light gray eyes of a West Indian.

Barnes turned his ferocious attention to the next man.

"Round shapes," said Lem, in a calm voice. He was older and stocky, had come from the deep South to Barnes's house, a shorter distance than the other man. His soft Virginia voice was lined with solid belief in what he could see.

"And what else?"

There was a long silence.

"Junius?" Sharply now.

"Overflow of color overtones." The words tumbled rapidly out.

"Lem?"

Lem took his time. "Long—brush strokes, Mr. Barnes." His voice had deepened and slowed.

"Anything to add?" Barnes urged them.

After a moment of silence, in which Junius turned in mute appeal to his fellow worker, Lem pronounced the words, "The rhythms of the color masses." Lem then eased his hands into his overall pockets with an air of finality.

Barnes got the message that the recitation was over. His face worked with fatherly emotion, proud. "Good!" The workers were dismissed.

Anzia was astonished by what they said and looked again. She had only seen the stories paintings told. Renoir's *Maternity*—a peasant woman outdoors with her naked baby on her lap, one of the little baby hands reaching for his fat little toes, the other touching her breast inside the open blouse. Greedily he sucked his mother's nipple. Everything bursting with life— the little round kicking thighs, the milk-swollen breast, the mother's flushed face. But also round shapes. Color overtones. Brush strokes.

"I'd rather have these men come in overalls and look at nekkid ladies than anybody else," Barnes said to the four researchers, or rather to the air over their heads. "Rather have their spirits open to art than the damned highbrows."

Later he called other Negroes in from places where they worked on the grounds and had them sing "Going Home to Jesus."

"The real thing," Barnes boasted. "No white spiritual claptrap or minstrel show fakes. Pure!"

During another of these visits, two distinguished-looking men arrived. Barnes had promised them a look at his collection. He called the four project researchers to the door and stood them beneath the sparkling chandelier.

"You wouldn't think it to look at them," he said to the visitors. He was pointing to Anzia, Ellen, Emmet, and Irving. "They are afflicted with a most unfortunate contagious disease. My household and I have already been exposed to it. I wouldn't dream of endangering you."

The callers were furious. The bald one slammed a bowler on his head so hard they heard it knock his skull. They left without speaking, but Anzia's bones ached from the curses she imagined they muttered beneath their breath.

"They write every damn day," Barnes said calmly. " 'Oh, please, Mr. Barnes, it would be the pinnacle of my life if I could see your wonderful paintings!' " To his wife Barnes said, "Tell 'em what I write back."

"Oh, no." Barnes's wife was beautifully dressed in green silk. She seemed to shrink inside her clothes. "It's funnier when you say it."

He snapped his attention to Marsh, who immediately, as if Barnes had issued an order, as if he had taken the words down in dictation often enough, put higher color into his florid face and said in one burst, "I'm devastated that I can't let you see my collection on the day you'll be passing through, dear Professor of Art. Three French poodles are scheduled to urinate in unison on the flower beds that day. The juxtaposing of live and dead plants will simulate the sculptured effects in the gardens at Versailles."

When Marsh stopped for breath, the researchers made little stirring movements. But Marsh, at some sign from Barnes not visible to the rest of them, was not finished yet.

"However, I'm open to requests from religious nudist colonies that wish to do penance among the Renoir nudes. Their self-loathing can carry them nicely through Lent."

Ellen, Emmet, and Irving all really did look sick.

"Or Dr. Barnes"—Marsh was immersed in his work, his big chest heaving with the effort to get everything out—"might offer to give a blueberry-pie-eating contest for members of the DAR without forks or bibs, just fingers. So refined. The prize would go to the woman who managed to get just one spot of berry juice on her paunch." Marsh had split his personality neatly

in two: he groveled before Barnes and showed a fierce, possessive arrogance in Barnes's behalf before everyone else. At any
moment Anzia expected that his excited voice would be thumped
by a ponderous sound from Barnes, whose single syllables could
fall like blows from a cleaver.

Instead, it was Laura Barnes who interrupted. She gave a
trembly ladylike laugh. "I think that's enough to give everyone
the idea."

"Who says it's enough?" said Barnes. For that he glowered
the rest of the evening, or maybe he would have anyway.

One evening there was a formal dinner to which an elegantly
dressed couple had been invited. While they all sat in the dining
hall at the great table laid with gleaming silver, the woman began a story about a slumming trip she had taken with friends to
the Lower East Side to buy lace.

She gave a clumsy imitation of a street peddler's accent: *vel*
and *vot* and *vere you vill get soch stoff?*

"I argued the price was too high," she said, "because you're
supposed to bargain with them. It's all they understand."

The woman played with her pearls in the low-cut bosom of
her gown. While she addressed the table, Anzia told herself to
let the woman talk.

"And then," the woman said, "he let out such a series of
wailings that my friends and I simply fled."

It was no use. Anzia overtook herself on the road, the head-
long companion she thought she'd left behind. "Wail? Why
shouldn't he wail? Did he have teeth in his mouth? Or a safe
place to sleep? Or proper food? Do you know what your pennies
meant to him?" Another outburst, when she had promised herself, No more!

After that, her lecture that no one paid to hear, the table
grew quiet. In a little while someone turned the conversation to
the war. Barnes sat silent, for once not taking over. Anzia had
trouble swallowing the meal. Not just the thick roast beef; even
the peas wouldn't go down. Moving from the table to what they
called the drawing room, she mentioned to Barnes's wife that
she was not feeling well.

"You'll want the powder room," said Laura Barnes, and
walked with Anzia in that direction.

"You're not afraid"—Laura Barnes was looking sideways at her—"to express what you feel. I was that way once."

"You don't know the half of what I'm not expressing," Anzia answered. Just walking away from the table had helped, and she was feeling better by now. She said she could rejoin the others, and the two women continued walking, passing through an alcove hung with tapestries and shielded with a red velvet curtain.

"If I ever went out into the world," Barnes's wife confided, pausing before parting the curtain, "I'd be eaten alive in two seconds, Albert says. I'm not even a very good hostess, it seems, though I was brought up to be one." Her eyes filled with small shining tears. Even her crying was stylish. "I am not a crier," she said with a flash of staunchness, "or a confider either. I was brought up to show independence of mind. But now—I make mistakes. I get so—unnerved, sometimes, when Albert's impatient with me. He is sometimes an impatient man, but of course he's a genius, so I understand how irritating it is for him when I get anything wrong. Sometimes I just mix up painters' names. There's no reason—just that I get nervous and I hear things wrong. Once I heard some guests talking and I said, 'Oh, peignoirs, I adore them; I have two hanging in my clothing closet right now.' Albert was furious. It wasn't peignoirs they were talking about, it was Renoirs. Of course I know Renoir, so why should I get it wrong? But I do sometimes. Maybe even tonight, you'll see. Something always happens."

"Tonight," Anzia said, "there are mostly only hungry students here who don't even understand what's going on."

But Laura Barnes was right. The next minute the red curtain was pulled open from the other side with a startling clang of its rings on the brass bar. Barnes glared through the opening.

"I said we'd have coffee, not goddamn demitasse! Can't you get the cups straight? Even my dog knows how to pick out the right bowl!"

Barnes's head vanished, and his wife, without even a parting look at Anzia, hurried away in her satin shoes, head down, her pleated gown making little gasping sounds.

Almost at once, Harry Marsh appeared within the curtained alcove, where Anzia still stood transfixed. He placed his hands on his hips and assumed a straddling stance on the rich

Oriental rug while he delivered his message: "Anything that happens in this house, if you're a guest here you keep your mouth shut, understood? You see my meaning?"

"I see," she said, though her voice was shaking, "your employer only knows how to value a woman if she's dead and hanging on the wall!"

Marsh stared as if someone claimed she was worth something and he was cataloging for Barnes, looking for flaws or a forged signature. His eyes were boiling like tar. Their resemblance to Barnes's eyes was startling, now that he was angry. She turned herself a little, so she wouldn't have to see his face, and made herself go on. "I see that he craves art because he can't bear what's human!" Then she closed her eyes and hoped for the best. The best would be that when she opened her eyes again she would find herself alone. But when her lids lifted, it was as if all this coming and going and whisking away of the velvet curtain had been like a magician's pass with a conjurer's cloth: now it was Albert Barnes who appeared before her. She shut her eyes again, hoping for a magical disappearance—either of him or of her.

"Why is it"—Barnes spoke in a voice so low she almost didn't catch words—"I can't paint but you can write? Why in you and not in me?" Then she felt hands moving over her: breasts, belly, hips. "What have you got in you? What put it there? Why in you, not me?"

Why don't you run now? she demanded of herself. You who never stay in one place, who nailed you to this one? But she stood fixed like a piece of sculpture. When she could do it, snap open her eyes and break out of herself so she could run toward the others, there was no one with her in the alcove.

As soon as she entered the salon she saw that neither Marsh nor Barnes was there. After a moment Barnes entered with his measured tread and forbidding look.

"And now," said the woman guest with excitement, "for the pictures in the special salon!"

In a moment, Harry Marsh came bursting in, looking wildly around like a dog that has temporarily misplaced its master.

Barnes bared his teeth in a frightening smile. "I'm devastated. But not tonight," he told the woman.

The guest turned pale. "You promised!"

116

"I can hardly help it that a rare fungus has attacked the canvases," Barnes said, his voice full of mock concern. "Human exhalation is its ideal growing solution. I wouldn't want your poor lungs, the very breath in your body, to bear that guilt."

For a single moment Anzia let herself imagine that the episode in the alcove, when Barnes had paid her the compliment of his envy, had brought them into some closeness that put Barnes on her side against the guest. She is repaid for her meanness, Anzia thought, but what an accounting system they keep here! She shuddered at the power to make such payments. Barnes can afford to pay back anybody, she thought, with ten times the pain!

It occurred to her, finally, that Barnes might have dealt this blow to the woman not because he was on Anzia's side at all but only because he was seized with some passion—anger or jealousy or whatever it might have been that led to the surge of energy and rage.

When at last the four project researchers could leave, Marsh, with a servile eye on his master, tried out a pleasantry at the door. "Shall we have everybody searched, Dr. Barnes? Any sticky fingers here?" His jokes were like punches from heavy fists. Barnes coldly ignored him.

But as they were moving away from the house, someone's voice—it was hard to tell whether it belonged to Marsh or Barnes—called out to them. They all looked back. The figures of Barnes and Marsh filled the doorway of the house.

"Better put it back," the voice called out to them, extending the joke, as they climbed into Barnes's car.

What back? Anzia wondered, pacing her room for hours that night. Gift? Talent? Put it back into the world so Barnes can have a chance at it? Was it Barnes, in fact, who wanted that? Had he been the one who said it? She kept going over the evening's scenes in her mind and wondered now if it really had been Barnes with her in the alcove. Or might it after all have been only Marsh? How could she not know for sure whether it had been Barnes or Marsh? Was there some influence at work in Barnes's house that made you make mistakes, like Laura Barnes, suddenly mixing up peignoirs and Renoirs when she certainly knew better?

Whoever it was, had he said, "Why can't *I* paint?" or "Why

can't *he* paint?" She was no longer sure even of that. It made all the difference. Even if it was "Why can't *I* paint?" did that mean it was Barnes who had said it? And who was it who had— she could hardly bear to bring that part of it into focus now— passed his hands over her body as if she were a piece of sculpture, an owned object? Couldn't that have been Harry Marsh, asking about himself? Like master, like disciple—if Barnes wanted to paint, probably Harry Marsh did too. But did Barnes want to be a painter? Maybe it was Barnes saying, "Why can't he paint?" meaning Harry Marsh, why couldn't Marsh be a painter, then Barnes could collect his work as well? Or could "he"—suddenly this struck her—have meant John? Why can't John paint? In that case the answer was easy. John is a poet. But that was secret. No one must know. Except that now Kaplan knew, or suspected, probably. She didn't want to think about Kaplan, king of the critical beasts, so she went back to Marsh-Barnes and "Why can't I/he paint?" Was Marsh mourning the lack of painter's gift in Barnes? Or Barnes in himself? Or Marsh in Marsh, or Barnes in Marsh? Soon she gave it up, and fell exhausted onto her bed. There were more hungry lions sniffing at art and ready to devour it, one way or another, than she could bear to think of.

16

White Chickens and a Red Wheelbarrow

John was waiting in painful tension for Kaplan's visit and judgment. Now and then, though, his mood leaped up to a level of confidence that encouraged them both. "I wrote those poems fervently enough, God knows, Anzia. They were like some seizure. I felt glaciers were melting." He lay back, suddenly languid, pressing his cheek into her pillow, where Philadelphia heat melted a few drops of moisture into the muslin.

"I know they were," she answered with her whole heart. "And Kaplan if he's any good will feel that!"

But if your sea starts freezing up in youth, Anzia thought, the first thaw will come from there. John's poetry was going to have to bubble a long time before he'd be able to skim off anything like a soup whose richness and texture matched the maturity of his mind. Would Kaplan take that into consideration?

"The trouble is," John said, "I'm starting to form Kaplan's judgment for him. I suspect what it will be. Not favorable."

When new poems shaped themselves now he heard the lines with Kaplan's ear. A peculiar sneering echo to the ecstasy of creation. A strict and ruthless judge, Kaplan. Impeccable.

After his visit to Kaplan, John had made another one, to the farm in Huntington. He wandered among the fowl, throwing

119

out corn. The sky was a blue painting. The chickens gleamed white. The empty red wheelbarrow, at rest, slanted toward earth. So much depended upon its humble function. Someone with the gift, he knew, could make a poem even of such simple things.

A rooster had flapped onto a hen, and a line of verse straddled his brain.

> *Old cock, fallen Icarus*
> *Let her warm center be thy sun. . . .*

He told Anzia how an echo (he was listening with Kaplan's ear) had mocked the line: fallen cock, licked Icarus.

His own children who gathered at the farm for the summer bewildered him. Fully formed men and women, they were set in their ways like people three times their age, older than he was. In the middle of dinner—full-breasted baked chickens from the farm, fresh-picked hot corn rolled in butter, and crisp snap beans he had helped to gather himself—he slipped back in his mind twenty years, to when the children were lively, noisy, and full of promise. His daughters and sons then used to troop into his corner, taking hold of his hands. "Come on, John! Stop thinking now and play a game." He would let them pull him. Alexander taught him now that when posture is poor, parts of the body are lagging behind others, showing the spirit's reluctance to commit itself to the life into which it's been dragged.

"My posture tells the story, Alexander says," John said to Anzia, pressing his heated cheek into the pillow with hers. "The only time there's no reluctance in me is when I'm with you, Anzia, and when those poems come at me."

In her mind's eye, Anzia pictured a lion roaring on the plain. She became a hunter: raised her rifle, took deadly aim, and fired.

17

The Tree of Knowledge of Good and Bad Painting

The trees flew by on the road to Merion when Barnes's driver next came for Anzia. Fired! Fired! they signaled. Fired from the project now John's not here.

John had left Philadelphia again, off to New York. Alice was about to make a visit to San Francisco and wished to confer with him. If it wasn't the farm in Huntington that took John away, it was Alice in the city. The counted-on continuity of Philadelphia days and nights was eluding them.

This time when I get to Merion I won't say anything to Barnes. Anzia vowed. It was easy to practice silence in the car. The driver, a slight, pockmarked man, never responded anyway to efforts at conversation, but homed like a horse to its stable.

When they arrived at the great house in Merion, Barnes himself greeted her at the door. His look seemed different, his face less dark. Marsh, the secretary-bodyguard-cataloger, she was glad to see, was not present. It was soon clear that she would not be fired from the project that day.

"Have a glass of wine," Barnes said. "Shall we look at some Renoirs? What, as an artist yourself, is your opinion of the placement?"

Taken by surprise, Anzia clung to her shawl, not allowing

the maid to carry it off. A traveler in a storm better not trust to a milky sun, she warned herself.

"No wine, thank you," she said, her voice sounding firmer than she felt.

Soon he was gliding beside her, his feet silent on the carpet, giving her a private showing of his paintings and watching to see her response. Orange flowers in the grass, no more than a squirt from a tube, springing up like tigers in a jungle. A man and woman at a table, her hand on the wineglass, his on the bread, their looks feeding on one another.

Anzia couldn't stop her mouth altogether and cried out once that it was like seeing God's creation. Then she cringed in her shawl, waiting for his sneer, but this time it never came.

"Three things last," he said gravely. "Art, if you're good enough. Money, if you're shrewd enough. Grievance, if you keep faith with yourself and don't forget a thing."

"I want to be good enough," she said. It was the only one of the three she cared about.

"You'll have to figure that one out." He had a way of holding his cigar—horizontal between two fingers and the thumb— and contemplating end to end, examining with a sharp critical eye. When he was through, he jammed one end between his teeth. She shuddered and thought of Morris Kaplan.

Finally Barnes brought her to look at a tiny painting, no bigger than a hand, brilliant as a jewel under the light. A woman standing naked in a little bathtub, just raising her leg to step out, a tissue of toweling about her hips. Orange-gold light poured over the wet satin of her skin.

"I want you to have this." Barnes was scowling slightly, not looking at her. "Keep it in your room."

When she was speechless too long, he glanced at her face and waited in demanding silence.

"Can't," she gasped, "it's too valuable!"

"Don't worry, not to keep. Call it a loan." He seemed already bored with the idea, so that her own awe embarrassed her. She stammered that it was too valuable even as a loan. He was forbidding, remote, distracted. Sometimes like John, but so different from John. Barnes in his distraction was carried to some region of ice. Why would he want her to have the painting?

"You want me to have it," she tried out, "to learn something, is that it?"

He nodded slightly, studying the pictures on his wall.

She went on suggesting reasons. "Do you plan for each of us to have a turn—Ellen, Emmet, Irving, me? Only you're starting with me first? If I look long enough I'll take in what makes a good painting—or what doesn't?"

After a delay, another silent shift of the heavy head that might have been a nod.

"Anyone who lives with such a masterpiece will *have* to learn something from it—that's what you mean?" She was nudging herself toward acceptance. She could feel resistance to Barnes's gift melting. If she had the little painting . . . if she could learn something and then offer it to John . . .

With all Barnes's other traits, there was still this, how generous he could be. John had tried to tell her. First Barnes had to pounce and pull down. Then after he roared over you he might come and give some rough licks to your face with his tongue. And after that he might deny all kindness and say he was only tasting your blood.

Why were lions always coming to mind?

"Thank you," she said quickly. "I will accept this generous loan."

"Not a word," Barnes warned, full of intense concentration on her again. "John's sense of fairness would make me give these out to everybody right now if he knew, and it's not what I've got in mind. Remember, keep it in a drawer, where the others won't see. Study it yourself."

Take it and not mention it at all, did he mean?

"Don't mention it to anybody."

What astonished her more than Barnes's behavior was her own. She took the picture and hid it in her drawer. She loved to look at the painting and study its lines. Why do I keep this up? she asked herself, as days went by and she said nothing to John when he returned. She felt herself to be in a conspiracy with Barnes.

Anzia began to copy out entries from her Philadelphia journal, whenever John was away, and save them for him. In this way, she told herself, I am doubly giving myself to John to make up for what I am withholding from him. Sometimes she stood at her window and thought, Do I even know whether John sometimes visits Barnes without coming to see me? Other times she went over in her mind how their love had sprung up in collision as they ran toward one another from opposite ends of the world. As different as the divisions in America itself—North and South, East and West, rich and poor, old stock and immigrant. And each of them divided again within—old self from self-that-wished-to-become. By the heat of our own desires, we soldered up those wounds!

Then again she would sometimes feel in herself a languor, a willingness to do nothing but wait in her room for John, sit in a chair by the window or lie on her cot facing the door. It was because of that she had to throw herself into motion. She carried the little painting with her one morning to the Piruszkis.

"You see?" Anzia propped the canvas against the washtub where Mrs. Piruszki would be sure to look. The beautiful naked woman stepping from the bath, her body lovingly brushed into being by the painter's hand, gleamed at them. With rough hands, Mrs. Piruszki parted the hank of hair that hung before her eyes.

Meanwhile Anzia slipped onto the kitchen table Sanger's circular, which she had translated into Polish.

MOTHERS!

Can you afford a large family? Do you want more children? If not, why do you have them? Do not kill, do not take life, but prevent. Tell your friends and neighbors. You will be given safe, harmless information from trained nurses.

Was that, Anzia asked herself, such a terrible message to bring to a woman worn out with bearing a baby every year?

"You see how valuable, how important a woman can be, just for herself? Imagine it! Not only this one—hundreds of others. Painters copy her form. They frame her in gold. Precious. A millionaire buys it. He keeps it safe, locked away."

Mrs. Piruszki peeped from behind a rag of steamed hair.

Was she seeing a creature in a zoo? She looked as if she might be counting arms and legs.

Suddenly, a commotion! Three men rushed in, the husband, the brother, and the brother-in-law. They jostled in the doorway, staring. Then they began to throw pieces of clothing at the tiny canvas. All to cover up a few peach-colored swellings. The husband threw his cap. The brother took off his sweat-stained shirt and threw that. The brother-in-law went further. He removed his undershirt and pitched it at the picture, leaving bare his thickly matted chest. A powerful smell of sweat welled like a wave, crashed over their heads and nearly drowned them. The way the orange tones crept around the edge of the canvas and brought the eye back to the center didn't interest them. They didn't see shapes or rhythmic masses. All they saw was Naked—a round buttock, a lifted thigh, a breast that poked forward as if to test the water with its nipple tip.

Mrs. Piruszki ran from her kitchen and hid. Alone with Anzia, the men, panting, glared with triumph, having shielded the woman of the house from the sight of her own flesh.

That night, Anzia began a note to John that described the powerful little painting Barnes had given into her care. But before long she was doing what John so often had done, disliking her own words and crumpling them, page after page, to the floor.

18 ···≼

Poetry's Thick Feet

The shakiness of John's faith in his poems was catching. Anzia berated herself: Why must everything depend on someone else's word? What's the matter with our own opinion? Why only Kaplan? And why only—it came over her in sudden inspiration—in English?

Without telling John, she sat down and wrote out all his poems she could remember. She must have omitted words, even whole lines, but at the moment it didn't matter. Most of the night she spent in a fever of translation, the English of John's poems into the Yiddish of her youth. Certain words appeared often. Heart *(hartz)* and burn *(brent)* and soul *(neshuma).*

In English, John had written, for example:

> *Flames of my heart yearn toward you,*
> *And my soul tears out of my breast in search of you.*

When Anzia translated the lines, they came out more Jacob than John, a good thing for her purpose.

> *Ich hob a hartz vos brent noch dir,*
> *Un reist mein neshuma arois fun mir.*

She took a day off from Philadelphia, made her way to New York by train, and to the Lower East Side by trolley. Abraham Cahan was as usual too busy to see her. She spoke instead to a short, skinny man in shirt sleeves and vest, sweating, tottering from overwork, an assistant to an assistant to the editor and not pleased to see her in that noisy, crowded, manuscript-stuffed newspaper office.

Anzia spoke up for John with a boldness she never managed here for herself.

"Count yourself lucky," she told the exhausted little man, "to have such poems in your hands."

He wiped sweat from his print-smudged brow and asked with sarcasm, "And who is this po-*et?*" He gave an old-world pronunciation to the word.

"His identity is secret."

"Secret? Here we don't publish Anonymous. Who ever heard of an anonymous Jewish writer anyway? They would kill their mothers to be published."

"He is not a Jewish writer."

The assistant's assistant looked astonished. "So why do we want him?"

"He is important to Jews. To all mankind, but especially if they are immigrants."

Even an assistant's assistant likes to put two and two together to make a joke. "Is he, maybe, involved with one Jewish immigrant in particular?"

Without another word Anzia handed over the pages, and without another word, standing before her, the assistant assistant editor read the poems. While he shuffled through the sheets she thought of Kaplan doing the same.

Not even halfway through, he let out a sound. "Pfui!" He nearly spat. "Why do you bring me such garbage? I'm thankful to hear he's not a Jew!"

"Don't judge so hastily." She began to plead with him as if he were Kaplan himself. "It must be my translation. Let me try again."

"If you put the first word last and the last word first and you changed every word in between, it would still be garbage. Don't you read, don't you know what we publish here? I will acquaint you. And I am translating, mind you, from Yiddish as I go."

He grabbed a sheet from the tangled pile on his desk and began, with an emotion-filled voice, to recite:

> *How feet make our hearts tremble!*
> *Light women's feet that fly past.*
> *But I love only those that are . . .*

He paused, he felt his fingertips with his thumb. "*Umgelumpert* . . . that's . . . that's . . . I don't know, clumsy, thick, but it's not the same . . . all right, never mind . . . *nu* . . .

> *I love feet that are thick and coarse.*
> *They remind me of good friends and old letters*
> *And of her who gives us life!*

"I am not myself a poet." The assistant's assistant wiped his glasses, misted over with emotion. "But Zisha Landau is, and I tell you, this is a poem!"

A mist came into Anzia's eyes as well. For Landau's poor clumsy feet and for John's poems, whose beauty she had not been able to squeeze into Yiddish. She had a horrible feeling that Kaplan might say it had not been squeezed into English either.

19

A Visit from
Mrs. Hut Spahdyk

The next time John returned, he was in pain. His old tension troubles had come back. He held his neck—or his neck held him—in a rigid position. If he turned or tilted to one side or another, rays of fire shot down his shoulder and arm.

He went first to Merion to see Barnes, and this time he could not leave. The punishing spasm in his neck muscle clenched itself too tight to permit him to take the short journey to Anzia, who waited in the house on Richmond Street in Philadelphia.

Barnes's generosity to John turned his big red-roofed house into a clinic for his recovery. A whole room of rich stuff—tables from Germany (from before the war), chairs from England, rugs from Turkey, crates of wrought-iron hardware from some castle in France (not to mention sculptures and paintings waiting to be hung)—were all shoved aside to make space for John and his sick neck.

Each day Anzia mailed something to Merion for John. She copied out pages from the fresh journal she had begun in Philadelphia, going back through weeks of time to the start of summer. She sent descriptions of a ground-floor sausage store—ropes of meat like entrails in the window, a blood smell seeping through the doorway. She described Cramp's, the munitions plant on the river that recruited its workers from the Polish community: the belching smokestacks, the air-piercing shift whistles. Once, before tearing up the page, she allowed herself to grumble: "Philadelphia defrauded us. The idyll was a lie. Eden was impossible in Barnes's backyard. How was it better than New York? We couldn't snatch more than moments in my room in Polishtown or on the riverbank."

But mostly she wrote about lovemaking. She painted word pictures of the secluded, grassy spot on the riverbank where they had lain together on her shawl in the moonlight. Anzia was inside the past, copying from it. Reading, John would be in the past with her. That way, she hoped the future would find them both in the same place. Now and then she squeezed in, like a dab of bright color, a cheerful note about growth and change to please his eye. "I miss you, miss you! But till we're together again I can experience new things, I can grow. I'm learning another city in America, because of you!"

Philadelphia. Feelaswelteria. She brushed away the drops of perspiration that fell here and there, tincturing her words with water.

Everyone in the Merion house knew about the mail that arrived daily for John from Richmond Street. When Anzia's letters came, he opened them in his lap without looking down. Then he raised his arms to eye level, so he wouldn't have to tilt.

She wished he hadn't taken all his poems away, Anzia wrote, even though she could say some of them by heart. *Not the same as ink on paper your hands have touched.*

Call them back from Kaplan, she wrote. *He won't know how to read them.*

She thought of writing to Kaplan herself to make him understand about John's frozen seas. But how could he—a reader of John's great works on education? What John wrote about in his books was the building up, by each experience, of inward growth. Who you are determines who you become. Who you are mixes with life and changes the experience that changes you. Anzia thought of a mosquito sucking out blood and pumping in its saliva, back and forth. Swelling and burning, that's good; that's change and growth.

Now John wanted reversal, overthrow, transformation. Mind

to heart, thought to feeling, intellect to body, make them become not two things but one, and then make them act on life so as not to lose a drop of anything, blood or spit. Could Kaplan understand that?

She slept badly, her nights dream-broken, and wrote what she dreamed: her sister knocking at the door, scaring her, making her think of bad news from home. "I have two things to tell you." Blowing on her boa and looking sly. "One good, one bad." She was getting married, but to a man no one could see. He was a wonderful man, but invisible to everyone but her. "So will you tell Papa for me?" Anzia rushed to his door and realized she didn't know which was the good news. Her father seemed well; a woman was taking care of him, giving him tea in a glass with two big pieces of sugar and a thick slice of lemon, though it was wartime.

"Your daughter is here."

"I can't see anyone."

Suddenly a huge animal like a bear walked through the doorway on its hind legs, giving horrible growls. Anzia woke drenched with sweat, burning up in Philadelphia.

My mother, when she lived [she wrote to John] *read omens for her children in dreams. Tea leaves, playing cards. Without education she made sermons from stones. Now I'll read my own dream. You will come soon. Barnes will shut up his growling.*

She pictured John reading her reading of her own dream, then lowering his lids, so the others couldn't read what was in his eyes.

Her dreams roused his. He dreamed they were lying naked on the big bed in Barnes's guest bedroom. John's letters were scrawled because of neck pain, but he got someone, maybe one of the men working for Barnes—could it have been Barnes himself?—to post them.

In another dream he was cutting down a forest tree with a great two-handled lumberjack saw. He sawed one end, then ran around to the other side and sawed back. His shoes were big and floppy, his pants baggy. He was a clown like Charlie Chaplin, sure to escape from the towering teetering tree. But he was caught. The timber was about to strike him across the middle, the saw leaping into the air to finish the job of splitting him in two. He awoke depressed.

When she thought about what they were dreaming, she asked herself if change could sometimes be sopped back up like ink into a blotter. What can I do to change the direction of change?

She had been picturing John in his chair, tall, curled over, his long fingers resting on the arms. Then she pictured another figure with him—herself.

Without asking permission, she borrowed clothes from Ellen Wright's closet. Ellen had so many suits and hats she wouldn't miss one outfit taken for a day. When Anzia had finished dressing herself in Ellen's fine clothing, she lowered a heavy veil over her face.

Striped summer awnings were out at the Reading Railroad Terminal on Market Street. Grateful for the shade, Anzia passed under them in her borrowed suit and shirtwaist and hat and continued to Broad, where she took the Pennsylvania Railroad to Merion.

At Barnes's door she drew herself up in imitation of the wealthy woman she had seen at Barnes's table. She informed the maid that she had urgent business with Professor Dewey, which could not wait. But then what she feared most happened. The maid summoned her employer.

Albert Barnes came to the door and looked her over.

"Mrs. Hut Spahdyk." She pushed her voice up high and barely moved her lips behind the veil, her notion of transforming into a wealthy Philadelphia lady with an old Dutch name. "I have come to speak with Professor Dewey concerning a school to which I wish to donate funds."

What did either of them know about Philadelphia ladies? That was Anzia's gamble. When Barnes saw she wasn't there to grab a look at his art, he left her standing in the hallway, then came back and allowed her in.

John was sitting in a chair at the window, before a desk piled with papers in disarray. She could see she had fooled even him.

"Don't you know me?"

She ran to turn the fancy brass door lock, then whipped off her flowery hat with the thick veil. Inspired by John's look of astonished joy, she whipped off next the jacket of Ellen's suit, then the long gabardine skirt, then the blouse with the lace jabot, and on and on till nothing was left. In that house full of naked women, she alone stood up with warm skin. *Dejeuner sur l'herbe*—a nude figure at her ease and a gentleman fully dressed.

When she climbed into John's lap, she felt his arms tremble.

"Is there much pain?" she whispered.

"If there's any pain now, Anzia, it isn't me that's having it. Dearest, oh, Anzia. . . ."

His caresses made her think that if he couldn't be a poet God should let him be a painter. His brush strokes seemed already perfected. "Get your poems back from Kaplan—please! Tell him you can't use any comments now."

Behind shut eyes he seemed to be agreeing to whatever she asked.

After a while they heard sounds of people beyond the door—knocking, talking, making a commotion. All those tight and heavy pieces of clothing had to go back on. By the time she had dressed and opened the door they could see the noise wasn't meant for them at all, it was only another case of rejected visitors to Barnes's pictures.

"Come back!" John called to her in a bold voice as she stood on the threshold. "We still have to discuss a transfer of funds."

Transfer of funds. That might be John's clever way of referring to his poems. Did it mean that he was going to ask for their return right away, without needing Kaplan's lion breath on them? Could that, she asked herself with hope, be it?

But Anzia (not Mrs. Hut Spahdyk) lacked the courage to go inside again in full view of everyone, shut the door, and become one of *The Bathers* a second time. She waved and went out instead as *A Lady Wearing a Veil*.

20 ···≼

A Philosopher and His Wife

It was Kaplan they waited for, but Alice who came. Someone (not John) had written to Alice (was it Barnes? was it Marsh?) about John's neck problem, the spasmed muscle that sent pain flaring down his shoulders, chest, and back, that kept his arms, grown so fond of embracing, clamped to his sides.

Alice cut short her California visit and now sat on a straight-backed chair next to John's pillow-propped one. Her hands clenched together in her lap, straining against each other as if to squeeze from them the response she hoped to eject from John.

"When it comes to attacks," she said, "let me remind you there are some far worse than the one on your neck."

She believed in duty, her own and others', and she practiced persevering despite pain. There were goads that had worked in the past. She was using them now to bring John around.

"Attacks in the press to be answered, John." She tapped a finger on a magazine article John had already seen in the weekly *Seven Arts.*

"Here's Randolph Bourne, John." Alice's voice was rising. "He's still a pacifist in spite of everything he knows, and now he's going after you because you had the courage to change your position on the war."

134

Her broad pale face became even paler when she was upset. The small features were losing themselves in the widening, flattening flesh.

John had known for a long time that Bourne would attack him. He was saddened to have lost his old friend to this political fight, but there were other losses to think of now. However, Alice was humiliated for his sake, and for her sake he tried to take an interest.

She began to read, her voice quivering with wounded pride:

> "To those of us who have taken Dewey's philosophy almost as our American religion, it never occurred that values could be subordinated to technique. His disciples are making themselves efficient instruments of the war-technique. There was always that unhappy ambiguity in his doctrine as to just how values were created—"

Alice looked up, biting her lip. "Unhappy ambiguity, John!" She read again:

> "It became easier and easier to assume that just any growth was justified and almost any activity valuable as long as it achieved ends. . . ."

While Alice read from her magazine, John stole looks at Anzia's letter, resting in his lap. She had copied from her journal a passage about a night when Barnes invited John to Merion. First, Anzia imagined it all as she walked by the river. How it was at the great table, with scenes of men and women, naked and clothed, in the vivid paintings hung all around. And afterward, when John came to her at the riverbank, how wild with wine and paintings and love he'd made them both. She'd had to lean against a tree to keep from falling down. . . .

Crack! Alice had rolled up the magazine and brought it sharply down upon the table's edge.

"And *then*," she went on, "he invokes the spirit of the dead and says that William James would not have allowed Pragmatism to fall into such abuse! So you are shamed and told that older brother William would have done better than you, nearly sixty-year-old upstart that you are!"

John raised distracted eyes.

"For God's sake, John!" Alice called him sharply back. "Don't let it all roll over you!"

He roused himself for her sake. Answered that he'd answer. On Alexander, too. "That misguided article! I know it, all right! It's of a piece with Bourne's attack on Alexander's book and my own introduction to it. For all I care, Bourne can call me stupid or evil. But not use me for attacks on Pragmatism. Or on Alexander."

"Bourne rushes about on his crooked legs like a hunch-backed crow in a cape. Naturally he can't believe physical condition is relevant to the spirit, John! How could he?"

He guided his words carefully past his lips, like a man carrying a match through rooms of sawdust. "Bourne's intellect is in every way free of his tragic physical condition. It must be the bitterness of war that's twisted him now."

And the bitterness of which war, he thought, had twisted Alice? He had never known her to speak so unfeelingly about a fellowman.

Sometimes John sat in one of Barnes's salons where Alexander, who had canceled a lecture tour for this, labored without success over John's spine and brain. "Forward and up, Professor!" boomed the voice so triumphantly restored to resonance by its own efforts. "You above everyone ought to understand. Aren't such movements of the spirit what you counsel to all Americans?"

After several days, Alice could bear no more. Sick of Barnes's house, she took John to a movie theater in Philadelphia. John looked longingly through the windows as they passed the familiar streets. Anzia. So near and yet so far. Pillows were carried. Barnes's car and driver waited for them at the curb. John hoped for Charlie Chaplin. The actor, half angel, half demon, fascinated him.

Instead, a caravan, burning sands, searing sun. John wondered if his longing for Anzia had finally carried off his brain to the tropics and made it boil over, like Gauguin's. Then he wondered if Alice had brought him to see a report on cholera in Arabia.

A woman languished of some pulmonary disorder, half fainting without medical attention on a couch strewn with fringed cushions in a tent hung with tapestries of Oriental design. A flap of the tent lifted. Another pulmonary sufferer staggered in. Bare chest heaving, he grasped at tent hangings for support and gazed at the afflicted woman. Her metal-lidded breasts rose and fell like the heated pot covers in Anzia's cooking class. Suddenly the man flung himself on the couch, on her.

The shock of impact struck John in the solar plexus. As the two pairs of lips before him met one another, the rectangle of the screen achieved a mathematical miracle: it became a circle which shrank, as if kissing lips sucked in their own substance.

Noises erupted from the audience. Cheers, clapping, stomping of boots, a few skeptical barnyard sounds. The tent, the couch, the exotic hangings, the desert sands were all snatched away, but not the longing he felt. Alice steered him from the movie theater.

"There! Now I've seen the wretched thing! The decorator told me all New York was bowing to the desert craze. 'Sheik is chic,' said this odious man to me. Now I can tell him I have seen it and scorn it."

Alice was still mysteriously irritated when they returned to their own bedroom in Barnes's house.

"New Yorkers are worse snobs than anyone in the country. Those women come into the parlor and say, 'How charming!' if you haven't got the draperies up yet."

She looked disdainfully at the sumptuous decorations of Barnes's house. "I could have lived content in shabbiness on a professor's salary as long as the children's education was good. You know that. But you're so famous now! Society ladies attend your seminar, carrying books to be autographed. They wish to call upon you at home!"

Jealousy in such innocent quarters astonished and saddened him. When all the while Anzia lived in the house—if Alice knew his imaginings—and shared his bed!

Alice veered and attacked from another direction. "When you answer Bourne, leave out the part about Alexander, John."

"He helps me."

"You say that clinging to your chair?"

She was attacking from all sides now. He ought to pity her.

Her unhappiness lay over him like a smothering blanket. He longed to throw it off, to return to Anzia's letter.

"You're taken in by him. He pretends to write what can't be talked about. Think your muscles and bones into patterns! Why not tell the circulatory system to run backwards?"

"His ideas fit our own on education. You never wanted to shy away from the unorthodox before," John argued, faintly.

He saw her neck and shoulders stiffen as if she'd caught his disease.

"I can't find proper teaching here on your precious East Coast, I can't work, and now you tell me I can't read! As for you—you are every exploiter's dupe! You go on and on—as I know you do!—in your correspondence with scoundrels and frauds. Anyone can engage your attention."

Perhaps Alice meant to complain of John's friendship with Dr. Barnes. But as they were in his house at the moment, she chose to name another man. "You allow Scudder Klyce, who pretends to be a philosopher, to scud over you, too, in his letters. You allow anyone to keep you from writing your books!"

She was dragging in every foolishness, even the correspondence with Klyce, a philosophy maverick, as if in that way to avoid mention of worse suspicions in her mind. She tugged, as she left the room, at a festoon of drapery, trying to pull down a curtain over this scene of bad acting.

(Was that, Anzia wondered, thinking in her room about John and Alice, how a fight between a philosopher and his wife would go? She couldn't swear to it. Only fill out with imagination the brief notes John sent.)

John had shown Anzia some of Scudder Klyce's letters. "If you do not avail yourself of somebody's help to get you out of your emotional stagnation," Klyce wrote, "and your confusion of what you are taking to be real with what you say . . . you are taking to be real, you have badly failed as a philosopher, and it would be very much happier for you and for others if you had never been born."

John kept the correspondence up. Even a maverick or a madman, he thought, might tell him some truth about himself.

After Alice left him alone, he reached into a pocket for a scrap of paper, a stub of pencil. Because Anzia's letter was in his lap, he felt her presence in the room. For the moment oblivious of pain, he began to write.

> *In the swollen heat of earth,*
> *My hot desires are given birth!*
> *In the tropical torrents that lap at my limbs—*

Abruptly the jet of poetry stopped. Silent in the silence, he waited, hungry for more. Then he remembered: Kaplan's verdict was still not in. He put away paper and pencil.

Meanwhile, Alice was remembering something else. She returned to the room and without transition made an announcement.

"I want us to adopt another child, John."

The suggestion stunned him. Years ago they had adopted a poor orphan boy they'd found in the streets of Italy. He had become their dear son, after poor Gordon died of childhood illness. But they had been young parents then, surrounded by their large brood of children. This pathetic suggestion by Alice did more to carve her unhappiness into his heart than any complaint. He searched for some plausible answer that would spare her an outright refusal.

"This will seem unjust to you, Alice. You're in the prime of life. But I—I am too old."

"You and I are just about the same, John!" She was at first sharp, but then she went on more dryly, "You'd be as good a father now as you ever were."

"I believe the risks at this age are too great, Alice. In my case, in my case alone—"

"Oh, John, genetic gallantry! It's too much!" But for the moment she let it rest there.

He had told Anzia, once, that he'd pushed all his feelings for safekeeping inside his armor. Now the suit of armor was off and the feelings were out. He couldn't shove them under any more, and he couldn't bat them away as if they were just so many flies—his neck hurt too much for him to swing an arm. They were swirling everywhere. Pain for Alice. Pain for him, terrible remorse, and the hot longing, still, for Anzia, above whose head pain was now poised to descend.

He could just about lift the handbell for help when an urgent need to urinate overcame him. This time the dam burst before help arrived. A couple of Barnes's workmen set about peeling off his clothes.

He was ashamed to be the duty they were assigned to. "So damned sorry you fellows have got to do this."

They murmured at him reassuringly, then kept on with their low humming, as if melody was their fumigation of the world. They had a hard time changing him. The soaked pants clung to his wet skin.

"Like everything else in this world," John said to them sadly. "Hanging on to what they know best."

21

The Shared Secret

Years later it seemed mad enough to Anzia. How she kept sending her journal entries to John, even with Alice there. How she wanted to give John faith in his poems somehow, while he waited for Kaplan. How she thought she could heal him long-distance, mailing him words from her Richmond Street room.

Even their most intimate times together—she brought them onto her pages. How some nights it rained and there was no walking to their favorite spot at the riverbank. How they embraced instead in her room, cheating its heat with their fever.

John allowed her envelopes to warm his lap for a while before he opened them. He wrote back—the letters formed with slow and difficult strokes—that dreams kept floating up. Once a large Chow trotted into the room and stood panting. Its black tongue lolled from the side of its blue-gummed jaws. The deep coat puffed and shook, coppery fire. The tail was flipped, acrobatic, above its back, revealing the puckered pink-and-black anus. The animal sank to the carpet, staring awhile from deep-set eyes. Then, to the dreamer's dismay, it stood and left the room. "Has my animal self departed from me?" John wrote.

Other times, of course, he dreamed of Anzia, lying naked on bright tapestries at the river's edge.

One day she took up her pen to write John at last the secret she had kept too long: Barnes had given her a treasure of a painting to look at for a while. She meant to say that she despised Barnes's warning to keep it from John and wished she had never followed that warning for even a day. She hated the secret. What pleasure could there be in any gift from Barnes that was not shared with John? That was what she meant to write. But something else came onto the paper.

> *If anyone told me I would want this* [Anzia wrote to John], *I'd have laughed to keep from crying. Now I can't wait for a time to tell you, one night while you're reading new poems to me. "These are the child of our love," you'll say. And I'll answer, "This child is the child of our love. Our old struggles will be healed in it. It will never grope for balance as we've done."*

If the worst happens, Anzia thought, and Kaplan tells John he's no poet, he'll read this and feel like a creator just the same. If the news makes him happy, we'll find a way to work everything out. If not, I'll say I made a mistake. I'll manage somehow alone. I'll go away and have the child and never tell him. She felt the rush of her blood. Her face burned. The energy of the challenge choked off any chance of thought.

The next second a terrifying vision of what such a life would be blew up before her like a blood-red moon looming from the river. Her pen clattered to the floor. Reaching down, she knocked over the ink bottle. She ran for a rag and sopped at the medicinal-smelling black pool at the edge of her table, a thin stream of it dropping heavily to the floor like a snake.

When she finished, the table looked as if someone had written a bold message across the wood and then blurred it to dark, indecipherable strokes. The message, whatever it was, had penetrated the wood where no one could follow it.

She was seized by a craving to walk for miles in the streets until anxiety boiled away in the rhythm and sweat of her striding. Instead, she paced the small room, her heart pounding like a second life already within. But nothing was sure yet! She might be seeing signs that a child was on the way, or she might be seeing symptoms of nerves, her own version of John's stiff neck.

Finally she decided not to post the letter. She would take it to John herself at the first chance. But before that chance came along, John's note about Kaplan arrived.

The afternoon Morris Kaplan came to Merion he had only minutes to spare before returning to New York. He spluttered out his story to John in a rage.

"Your friend, Barnes! 'What is your schedule this week?' your friend Barnes asked me on the telephone.

" 'Kind of you to inquire,' I answered. 'Free in the afternoons. Except for Wednesday, when I'm scheduled to give a rather important lecture in the early evening.'

" 'Come Wednesday,' he said. Wednesday, it turned out, was the only day not filled up.

" 'Of course,' he said, 'if you'd rather not, if you find other engagements more pressing—'

"I had to assure him, then, that Wednesday, of course, would be fine. But I asked if I might come on the early side, on Wednesday.

" 'Come on the early side if you like,' he said. 'We will be ready for you on the late side. If it doesn't suit you—'

"So I had to spring to it again. No. Yes. Thank you. It's fine."

John's friend Kaplan fumed.

"Then he kept me, he kept me, it was cat-and-mouse. He must have seen me stealing glances at my watch. I was looking at the paintings and my stomach was churning the whole time, wondering if I was going to get to my damned lecture. Don't ask me what I saw. Then all of a sudden he tells me he's making his car and chauffeur available to drive me to my lecture in New York. So that's what I'm waiting for now, the final goddamn act of charity!"

"He gives and takes away, Morris," John said. "Takes away and gives back tenfold. He has devilish humors, but the generosity of an angel. In spite of everything, he's making treasures of art available to our countrymen. I believe he has an artist's soul."

"And *I* believe"—Kaplan was still in a fury—"that I know something about the rigors of art and the price an artist pays for them. I can tell you it never makes a man go rotten. When I see a son-of-a-bitch who's an artist I don't think, Look what art did to him. I think, Look at what by some miracle that bastard was able to do in spite of himself."

John's eyes, though he willed them not to, traveled at this terrible moment to the bundle under Kaplan's arm.

"Oh, yes, your other friend's work." With a violent movement as if swinging against some mortal enemy, Kaplan hurled the manuscript onto a desk, where it skidded and dwindled to rest.

"Tell your friend to turn to some other profession. And spare the world!"

John's note didn't have all that in it. It was no more than a few stoical lines. Yet Anzia saw and heard it all, everything, right down to the sickening squeak of the rubber band that held the manuscript together as it skidded across the wood.

Now, Anzia thought, it's time for me to let him know what we've created together. Even, oh, yes, even if Alice is there!

22

A Realigning

Barnes's driver picked up the four researchers at Richmond Street and took them to Merion, where they made some try at reporting activities to John. His chair was swung around to face them. With pain-darkened eyes he listened but said nothing. They huddled near the doorway of the room.

Alice, watching, sat with loose fists resting on the carved knobs of an armchair. Her long hair was newly bobbed, as if she had stripped herself down for this crisis. Gray strands darted from her head like live lightning bolts. Except for that electricity, and in her eyes as well, she sat like stone.

Anzia also felt darts of energy coming from her. She herself darted. Toward John. Carrying an envelope to which she had tied with string a cluster of ripe red cherries. She dropped envelope and cherries into his lap, then darted back to the doorway. She left the envelope unsealed, so he wouldn't have to struggle with it.

"It's short." She was breathless with daring and darting. "It won't tire you."

John kept his eyes on the envelope while his hand moved slowly toward his lap. Barnes and Alice had watched Anzia's movements. Now Barnes moved closer to John's chair.

"Maternity!" Anzia cried it out from the doorway with desperate inspiration. "Renoir's!"

"These women with their peignoirs," muttered Barnes, and scooped the letter from John's lap. "Too tiring for you now, John." He shooed the researchers away.

But later, when they were gathering their belongings to leave, Alice called to Anzia. "Stay. Please." She led the way to the alcove behind the red curtain, as if Barnes's house were hers.

Anzia's heart hammered her into a chair.

Silence.

Then: "John is fond of you."

How did she know that? Had John finally told her? Who else could have? Barnes? Why? Had Alice already seen the note Barnes intercepted?

Henry, you mean? Anzia wanted to say that. Alice and she must be inside one of Anzia's own stories. Everything else seemed unreal. They were Mary Morrow and Fanya. John was Henry Morrow. Anzia felt she could speak only from inside the stories, where endings turned out the way she wanted them to.

They sat very still. Anzia thought about which of Mary Morrow's characteristics should erupt now. Haughty ice? Break things?

Alice/Mary leaned forward. "You're young," she said kindly. Her next words were mysterious. "You can still bear other children." Suddenly Anzia heard her sisters' voices, demanding in their childhood game: Would you rather be Rachel or Leah?

Anzia's throat pinched off her breath—nothing got in or out. Rather be Alice or Anzia? With or without a child?

"Some men are considered to be educators. They contemplate the idea of the child in society and barely know their own. Yet they hold high positions in universities, they sit on important committees. Home is the married woman's university. Her committee meets in the nursery, without adviser or peer. There she teaches, unencumbered by fame or financial considerations, touching every fiber of the child's mind from birth. And is happy to do so under such terms."

Anzia's breath almost stopped. Another learning expert, powerful as John!

"But for this there must be a child in the home. When that

time is over a woman's position is gone. She is doubly without portfolio, dismissed without cause, stripped of university and committee connections, retired against her will and every inclination of her powers."

Alice looked as if she had slept in her clothes, a black bombazine skirt and a rumpled twill shirtwaist. She was stoical, separated from her own words. If she were in one of my stories she would show her feelings, Anzia said to herself, she would weep now. Instead it was Anzia who found tears painted over her vision.

Mary/Alice stared sternly ahead. "A child, anyone's child, your child, is a teachable entity."

My child? Does she mean Louise? Am I in my own story now and can't even cry for us?

Alice was silent for a moment. Then: "Think what it might mean to an immigrant's child to be brought up not in a ghetto but in the home of a great and famous man. I myself am not ignorant of pedagogic techniques. John and I have already adopted one child—we plucked him from an Italian square, shivering and homeless, and carried him away. Why shouldn't I do as much for any other, especially if . . . ?"

When she stopped, Anzia was shivering herself. Barnes let you see my note, she thought. But you can't pluck this one. Even if I'm right and there is one for plucking, I won't let you pluck it.

But before Anzia/Fanya could find words, the red velvet curtain rattled its rings.

"Don't forget she's got a husband who could be the father!" It was Marsh, Barnes's faithful assistant, red-faced with urgency. "These people are fertile as flies, don't we know that? Don't most of our sales come from ghetto clinics where Argyrol is used against *conjunctivitis neonatorum?*"

Marsh was addressing this to Alice, who at first sat rigidly silent, only tilted back in distaste, away from Marsh.

Barnes must have sent him, Anzia thought. He thinks I've invented some scheme to tie John to me. In the dizzying moment, she whispered to herself, I'll return Barnes's painting, as if that were the cause of all misunderstanding. Why didn't I do it long ago? She thought with horror of his reading her note to John.

"Are you mad? Have I," Alice said to Marsh, "asked you yet to speak your piece?" Alice's icewater voice woke Anzia from her storytelling sleep. Alice in Barnes's own house said to Marsh, "Get out and stay out!"

Anzia felt as if her blood was draining away, but all the same she thought with astonishment, now Marsh is paid back for all the ones he kept out.

"Or else"—Alice raised from its teakwood pedestal a jade sculpture of a Chinese lady in a narrow pleated gown—"I will let fall this treasure belonging to your employer, and let him know that I was forced to shatter it in response to your interference here."

Marsh's cheek turned even rosier. A Rubens buttock, thought Anzia, art-instructed, before Marsh disappeared in a clash of curtain rings and a shower of red.

Alice/Mary's voice went on as steady as before. "I understand you already gave one child away."

"Not gave! Not away!" That cry let out all Anzia's breath. The image of her daughter rose before her, in her little dress with the big sailor collar that she'd worn when Anzia was with her last. She raised her little arms to Anzia, who answered with her own arms upraised to her child. To Alice, watching, it was as if Anzia embraced a ghost.

Just then the curtain, clashing open, made Anzia gasp in air again. Someone grabbed her upraised arm.

"I want you—quick—for the Professor! To demonstrate how forward and up is not the same as ahead of yourself and gawking."

"Are you mad too? We are engaged here." Alice laid hold of Anzia's other arm.

Alexander looked past the end of his sharp nose at the two women. He inhaled deeply, and a clever light broke over his features.

"Ah! We have here a realigning. Very good. As with head, neck, shoulder, hip, ankle. As with nations. So with the ladies."

"Get out," said Alice. "Or I may have to write to *The New Republic* about the condition of my husband's neck after repeated sessions with your alignments."

"After each session he is aligned," Alexander answered hotly.

"My technique and I are not to blame if the imbalances of his life twist him out of shape!"

On springing heels, Alexander strode from the room. The red hangings clashed into place again. Anzia, moving past them too, on her way out, felt as if she'd brushed against something blood-soaked.

The next morning Anzia placed the painting on her bureau. No more hiding! Then she was going to speak to Mrs. Piruszki, alone, to repair the damage done at her last visit. The two acts seemed connected. After that, she swore to herself she would return the painting to Merion. And find John. Never mind the foolish idea of struggling with this all alone. Never mind if Alice wanted to have a child that would be half John's, never mind if Barnes wanted to keep Anzia from John, never mind how far Marsh was willing to go in carrying out Barnes's wishes. And never mind speaking in the language of painting titles.

"I'm going to bear your child," she would say to John directly, no matter in whose hearing. "Change your life for us, as I have changed mine for you!"

But when she returned to her room in the afternoon, the painting was gone.

23 ···✣

Human Nature and Conduct

"Portrait of a Woman with Wild Red Hair," she could have been called. And with mad eyes. If the police had bothered to call her anything but "crazy!" and "troublemaker!" while she gasped out claims to something the police knew she never had. No one who possessed anything of value looked like Anzia.

In the station house, everything was meant to overpower you—the heavy high sergeant's desk, the massive benches, the tall slope-topped column of oak filing drawers, all ink-bespattered as if brutal beatings had gone on until poor wretches had vomited up their words.

Anzia was spewing up her own confession to a stolid officer who wrote it with a slow pen. While she was trying to convince the police that a woman inside a frame had been kidnapped, another woman, framed by two policemen, was brought in. She was supported, nearly dragged, by them. One of her innocent blue eyes was blackened. Her lips were swollen to purple, and an angry welt ribboned her cheek. A sickening smell clung to her clothing, her torn and filthy jacket.

Anzia interrupted her own story with a cry.

"I know her—it's Miss Westerfield! She must have been attacked by the crowd. She ought to have medical attention right away, not be brought here. . . . Take her to a hospital!"

The patriotic police wanted no accusations. Every man in the street was a war worker or a soldier to them. The two women were themselves the unsavory characters.

"This one's here every week," said the sergeant at the station, pointing to Barbara Westerfield. "As for the other"— thumbing at Anzia—"don't she *wish* some man'd come into her room and steal something." His voice, on the last part, rose to a ridiculous imitation of a woman: "Stee-e-al something!"

Another patted his stomach. "Don't worry, girls. The boys'll be back soon and keep you out of mischief!"

They told Anzia she'd better get out or be locked up too.

Barbara whispered, "Do what they say. My friends will come to help." She whispered something else through swollen lips. "Never try to change people who don't want it." As if the street had taught more to her than she to it.

Anzia had flung herself face down on the bed and would not answer the nervous burst of knocking at her door. When it persisted for a long time, she said in a choked voice, "It's open," and Ellen Wright walked in. Her usual soft-spoken calm had shattered. She kept waving one long-fingered hand before her in Anzia's direction, a nervous beckoning and warding-off gesture.

"I want to tell you," Ellen said, "I want you to know I've taken the blame entirely upon myself. I came into your room for some translation. Do you see . . . ? How it really wasn't my fault . . . ? How anyone would have thought what I did . . . ? But I've taken the blame on myself all the same!"

"What are you talking about?" Anzia said. "Blame for what?"

"You were out, but I saw the little painting on top of your bureau. I knew it must have been sent from Merion for all of us to study. I thought it would be a wonderful bridge to students and teachers, where language failed, and took it along to the school. But it was snatched from my hands! Some of the teachers were enraged. I have no idea if it's still in one piece or if they ripped it to ribbons. Oh! what if they did?"

Anzia was pulling herself up to a sitting position. She looked uncomprehendingly at Ellen. "What do you mean? You took the painting? Why can't you answer yes or no?"

Yes or no couldn't touch the cascade of confession pouring out of Ellen. "I went at once to Merion to tell them. When I couldn't find Dr. Barnes or Harry Marsh, I spoke to Mrs. Dewey instead. I asked her to let them know and said to be sure and say that I'm the one responsible for the loss of the painting, because I took it, even though with the best of intentions, I'm the one who took it to the school."

Anzia sat without speaking.

Ellen said again, in a kind of ecstasy of confession, "You are free of blame, you should understand that." After a little pause she said uncertainly, "I hope you weren't worried." And after that, in a stronger voice, "I tell you, everyone knows you're not to blame!" When she left, she closed the door resolutely behind her, as if the positive attitude with which she embraced her contrition canceled all negative effect of her acts.

Pale as paper and pencil-thin, his eyes ink-dark, John came to Richmond Street.

"What have you done?" He stood in the center of her room, and as he spoke, the white of his cheek roughly reddened. Anzia had never seen him angry before. Stupidly she thought he must have learned anger from living in Barnes's house.

"I've done and not done so many things, I don't know which you mean. But whatever it is don't be angry with me, please. Just tell me how I've upset you. I don't want to do that, ever."

"During my illness haven't you spent private time with Al Barnes? Didn't he, who keeps his treasures under lock and key, present you with a costly painting? Isn't the meaning of all this clear? A priceless gift to you from Barnes?"

"I wanted to tell you. I meant to. It was a stone on my heart every day. I couldn't wait to be rid of it!" Anzia cried. "Who told you stories about my spending time? If it was Marsh, he's full of lies—he hates me or fears me or is demented, anyway, on Barnes's behalf—"

John ignored her outcry and said levelly, "Give it to me now, then. Show me that the gift and Barnes mean nothing to you."

"They mean nothing. But I can't give it to you. A terrible

thing happened—the painting disappeared and I didn't have the courage to tell Barnes. So Ellen did the telling, and it's all, all wrong!"

She threw her arms around his neck. With a short, brutal heave—she couldn't help automatically thinking, Thank God his strength has returned—he shoved her away from him. Her hip collided with the corner of her table, a pain she did not feel till later, when she saw the bruise in her flesh.

She hardly recognized him. The calmly beautiful face was not there now. Anger contorted it out of existence.

"This is not you," she said. "Is it because of Kaplan? Because of your poems? Because of the pain you've been suffering?"

Meanwhile she searched her mind for a glimpse of how a gift could goad him. Was it the passing between Barnes and her of the little naked woman? As if all nakedness were the same, and all could lead to nakedness in her bed?

John lifted his hands and let his face sink into them. "I can't begin to—"

At the same moment, she started to say, "Oh, please, let me tell you. . . . They didn't let you read my note!"

He shook his head. "I can't talk now." He spoke from behind his fingers. "If this is what passion does. . . . If desire draws such demons from me. . . ." When he raised his reddened eyes to look at her he asked, "Do you know how frightful it is to be unrecognizable to your own self?"

"Oh, yes, how frightening it is!" Anzia cried. "How painful! But it's one way for us to know, isn't it?"

His hands fell to his sides and he looked at her with a blank, exhausted gaze.

"To know," she said humbly, "that we are changing?"

He closed his eyes, his thin body swayed, and he seemed for a moment like a man praying. When he opened his eyes again he kept his gaze on the ground.

"I can't stay here, Anzia. You see that, don't you? I've only been able to come away for a moment. . . ."

It was not until he left that Anzia remembered what she held in her hand: a brush filled with brilliant color. She could stroke it onto the canvas and alter the picture. She could tell about their child. But not until John was himself could she tell him. The next day, wandering in a fever of restlessness about the city, she entered a bookstore so that she could hold John's volumes in her hands. *School and Society, Democracy and Education*. . . . He liked to give his books paired titles. She had grown used to the pairing of their own two names.

24

Cool Matter from the Stars

Night after night Anzia walked at the riverbank, hoping to pace her churning thoughts and feelings into some order. One night rain suddenly began to beat down. The earth rotted like fruit beneath her shoes. Mud squeezed up to her ankle laces, dribbling inside. A few boats on the river showed light, hooted like animals dying. Something like a wound smell came off the river, like a festering sickness.

Rain drubbed her shoulders like blows, but she ignored it. She was thinking of how John's anger would be washed away the moment he knew the whole truth. One terrible mistake she saw she had made was to wait so long for just the right moment to speak. She had come to think of their life together as a rich painting, and had wanted the canvas to call forth her strokes of truth in the right way—the shapes, the rhythmic color masses. What foolishness! What she hadn't considered was how much each of them had changed.

A letter wasn't enough any more. Things had altered in Barnes's house, and now Marsh or Barnes or even Alice might intercept it. Mrs. Hut Spahdyk would never work a second time, but for a moment she did consider stealing Ellen's clothes again. Should she take the hat with feathers and a veil and say that she was Mrs. Throckmorton come to see the paintings even if there was contagious disease in the house or fungus on the canvas? Or rub burnt cork on her face, say she'd wanted to learn about art all her life, and apply for employment as a maid? All she needed was two minutes! Bang on the door and scream for Alexander? I can't bend my neck! My hip, my leg! My back is narrow, my head is down, help!

All right. She began to walk faster. I'll do something. I'll do all of them. She was striding along in the rain, saying the wretched ruses over, half laughing at herself.

A new dark fancy occurred to her. What if, while she walked along this dirty river, some menacing figure rose from the gloom and smoke of the factory chimneys that burned all night? With no one near to help, would she run, scream, fight? This sick fantasy tilled up the terror she had tried to bury. All the while she was walking along the riverbank and planning—I'll do this, I'll do that, I only have to do something!—she had been trying to push away the fears that now flung themselves in her face like pelting rain.

The life with John that had come to such full fast flower, the perfume of it dizzying her, was now altering to something else. Not dying, no, she knew it wasn't that, but shrinking, bewilderingly, before her eyes.

Suddenly she heard conversation going on near her that she had been unaware of all this time. Behind her, men were talking. She caught, in the floating strands of Polish, words that made her think they were speaking of her, recognizing her.

The wet river wind, blowing at her back, carried to her nose the fumes of vodka and a blood-meat smell. Rising from the darkness before her a bloodied apparition, Barbara Westerfield, hoarsely whispered, "What the street teaches you!"

From behind a blackened tree, Levitas's weighty voice warned that she would pay dearly for forgetting the Jews of the Kishinev pogrom.

"Listen to me," said a voice of her own from deep within. "Run!"

She had walked for hours along the river and now would have to measure off that distance before she could come to the place where the riverbank turned off to the road. Along the soggy, bumpy ground, shoes sliding and twisting, she began to flee.

They're coming! No, they've gone! No, listen again! Still there, following! Above her pounding pulse she listened for the voices of the men.

For a long time she ran, her muddy skirt sagging and slapping against her ankles. One minute she was running; the next, her foot was in a hole, bent sickeningly backward. The shoe tip of the other instantly caught inside her hem. She went down. Then she heard nothing but her harsh breaths, her booming blood. At last, the silent lapping river.

Her body lay twisted, her face upturned to the needle points of rain. Before she could struggle to rise, two men leaned over her, their breaths heavy with the fumes of Polishtown.

"Why you run?" They braced their hands on the knees of their workmen's pants and shouted down at her as if she had fallen into a deep pit.

Then she was seized. Her elbows were grabbed, and in one swoop she was lifted from the mud and set upright onto her feet, one ankle wincing.

"Why?" they shouted into her face. "Why? Why run?"

She felt for the muddied shawl dangling from one shoulder and told them she thought she'd seen lightning among the trees.

They laughed, family men, acquainted with women's fears. "You stay home. Safe!"

Crossing their arms and interlocking strong fingers they showed how they would carry her. She thanked them. She said she could walk and then tried not to sway as she stood, watching them leave. They glanced back once.

Her thoughts took up the wild running left off when she fell. A clumsy Gulliver, you are! Tied to dirt by Lilliputian fears of your own making. So she'd ended falling and cribbed in mud, a border of it rimming her outline, as if the boundaries of physical self, mocking, had imprisoned spirit. Who was that woman inside—she searched herself for the answer—who made me run in panic? Was she realer than I? I am which one? Who? Where is my new life? Where is change? When will I be brave? Use the intelligence I have? When will my new life squeeze the old slavish fears from my soul?

She began to limp through the dark streets, past houses filled with sleeping families, past corner taverns still showing dim lights. Holding onto walls.

When the wringing in her belly began, she felt at first that she was expelling some old unwanted self. Then the wringing grew stronger, and she understood.

"Wait!" she whispered. "Don't take. Not away."

Because no one witnessed her heavy shuffle up the stairs—step, pause, creak of banister as she leaned into the wood—because the others had trained themselves to keep their doors shut, in her misery she thanked God she could not be seen or touched. She dragged herself to her room. There the wringing in her belly went on, as if some marauding animal were midwife, pressing her body between its jaws until the little life could burst out. At last what was in her of John and Anzia, the tiny mingled bit, escaped her like burning tissue seared from her own marrow. It was not, after all, composed of cool matter from the ideal region of stars.

She dreamed a white ship sailed. Not the kind that churned with sickness in steerage to America, not a troopship crammed with soldiers. No—a luxury peacetime ship, clean and comforting. It traveled east. She and John stood together at the railing. A breeze fanned their cheeks. His face was eager, his gray hairs lifted by the wind. Tenderness for him tore her heart. He gazed into the water: "A man ought to be like that, never at rest, like the ocean!"

She slept fitfully through the next day, and only Emmet knocked at her door to ask if she was all right. Afterward, writing in her journal, she took up the disguise of fiction, changed Anzia to Fanya, John to Henry.

Only if she made believe it happened to someone else could she bear to tell it. She printed in all the margins: DO NOT COPY FOR JOHN.

158

25

The Nature of "This"

All the same, Anzia knew John would come back, and he did. A few days later, they met in the downstairs room of the Richmond Street house that smelled of horsehair and damp. He had sent a note, naming an hour when the others would be out. She knew his anger would be gone, and it was. Instead of rough redness, pallor was on his cheek. He seemed chilled-looking, and his hands hung motionless at his sides.

Anzia had come into the parlor early and had stood waiting in the middle of the room facing the door. When John entered, he stood silently looking at her. She started toward him, believing this to be like the time in her room in New York when the kettle scorched and a little movement in his direction brought him hurtling forward, his arms catching at her like a drowning man's. But his voice halted her. It was low, faint.

"Forgive my outburst when I was here before," he said. "I was not myself."

A flood of forgiving words poured from her. "I know," she said, "I know that! And there's nothing to forgive, my dearest—"

He went on speaking in his low voice, as if not hearing. ". . . based on some madness, some terrible fantasy." He gave a disbelieving shake to his head, a small turn in each direction on the just-healed neck. His eyebrows raised themselves at the inner corners, as if pulled by pain. He lifted an arm toward her, but as she moved forward, he dropped it to his side and she stopped and was still. "The more fantasy, the better. I know that now. Anything at all to veil from myself the simple truth I wanted to evade."

She did not want to ask, What truth? He sighed as if she had.

His voice hoarsened as he went on. "You must know how grateful I am to you. You kept me from becoming the even drier stick I might have been if you hadn't found me. You must know that. What I would have been if you hadn't found me."

She had snatched her shawl from its hook, before running down the stairs, and was weaving and weaving at the fringes of it. If I must know all these things, why must he say them? What would either of us have been if we hadn't found each other! He must know that.

He pressed his long fingers against his mouth, stroking down his mustache with a small, sad, closing-down gesture from which little clumps of words escaped. "Pulled too many ways . . . work neglected . . . the body itself rebels . . . if pain is the end of so much joy . . ."

"You told me there are always ends beyond ends, ends are endless," she shot back. She had been through a great deal in recent days and had no time to waste equivocating.

"I no longer see where we are going. . . ." He looked at her with one hand shading his eyes as if what he saw in fact glared too brightly.

"You said the need for certainty was a refuge for the timid!" She was implacable, a font of quotations from himself, as if she had learned and learned only for this moment.

He tried again, weakly. "There is in you so little"—he searched for a word—"modification . . . of impulse. . . ."

The word seared in. She seized it and threw it back. "Modification! When did you ever say you longed for modification? Did you think you'd find passion in *modification?*"

He looked as if he could still consider the meaning of her words, even now. "You may be right. As always, Anzia. Maybe I'm only shunting from impulse to habit again, our other old pole star. Maybe. . . ." He began, ill and swaying, to deliberate.

She could not bear his cogitating upon their condition as if they were some abstract model of humanity. But at the look of pain that crossed his face, she softened. "You've changed in all the ways you wanted to change," she said with tenderness.

"Yet not changed enough, it looks like now," he answered, in the same somnambulist tone, as if communing with an elusive inner self. "Not enough to withstand this . . . this. . . ." In a near whisper he added, "I believe Alice knows about us. It might have been Marsh who accidentally let the word fall to her, or Al, all well intentioned." He paused before coming to a new point. "I destroyed the letters you sent me, but I've wondered if there was any rash thing in that note you left on your last visit, the one I never saw?"

He seemed then to be listening to his own breaths. His forehead broke into a net of fine wrinkles as he lifted his gaze to her. What were his eyes saying? Please, Anzia, teach me? Reach me?

Not caring if this time he threw her across the room, she ran to fling her arms about him. She kissed him on the mouth. Tears ran onto their lips. For one moment, he held her tightly. Then he placed his hands on her forearms, until she understood that he wanted to leave her embrace.

When they separated, she looked down at his shoes, wondering if his socks were mismatched today.

"Oh—think of your poems!" It suddenly burst from her.

He nodded wearily. "Yes, the poems. I took them to my office at Columbia, where I could read them over quietly, and saw for myself that Kaplan was right. They were self-delusion. I threw the whole manuscript, the whole lot of them, away." A trace of anger returned to his voice. "Why did you make me believe I could create poetry? That I, this dry stick, was a poet?"

"You could! You did!" She felt stunned. "How could you do that? Throw away—kill—your best self?"

Instead of answering, he said quietly, "What I need now, Anzia, is to have my letters back. I know you'll understand."

All the while she was stumbling up the steep wooden stairs, she was thinking of the thrown-away poems. In her room, she looked at the window. It glared hot as a sidewalk, and she felt herself tilt, almost lose her footing in the vertigo of displacement. The narrow bed. The stiff chair. Whose room is this? she wondered. What is this place? What is this that's happening now? What is the meaning of this . . . this . . . ? She smelled the river, the decay of its rain-soaked banks. She found the wool that would have stitched up his poems and, with fumbling fingers, tied the letters together.

When she came down again, John was standing in the same spot. He looked as if a blow had stunned him, as if he might fall if the stiffness of his joints and Alexander's "forward and up" were not holding him erect. Without a word she handed him the bundle of letters.

His chest began rapidly to rise and fall. He was straining in air, blinking like a man coming up out of water. He moved slowly backward. In the doorway he stopped. "Our riverbank . . . our Paris . . . our Eden," he murmured.

He seemed about to plunge forward again. Instead, he tossed a phrase into the room like crumpled paper.

"The poems went into the wastebasket," he said, "where they belong. And all this . . . this—" He lifted his hand in a gesture that seemed to take in the room, Anzia, summer nights. Then he turned away and left abruptly, shutting the door with finality behind him but catching the pocket of his suit jacket somehow on the tongue of the lock so that he exited not with a slam but with a ripping noise. Anzia never heard it. A stroke of pain blotted out sound and bent her to the floor.

In one of Dewey's lectures he spoke of the man who entered a room and announced, "My heart is bursting, it cannot contain all this!" About the man and his bursting heart Dewey mused aloud in the classroom, "What is the nature of 'this'?" Now Dewey has left the room. "This" has thinned and sharpened itself to a knife blade Anzia feels stuck in her heart. What is the nature of this? Did the apostle of experience—the "thisness" of life—withdraw from experience? Does Randolph Bourne's criticism of Dewey's philosophy—the one that so infuriated Alice—apply? Did Dewey really allow himself to think that "any growth was justified and almost any activity valuable as long as it achieves ends"? Do *unachieved* ends transform change into something inconvenient, or disturbing, or embarrassing, or bad for the philosopher's health? Is there any logic to upbraiding a man for abandoning a lover when he has already surreptitiously abandoned a wife?

What is the "this" we are left with? Are men and women like nations? Is their painful sense of "I-am-not-yet-complete" such necessary fuel to their burning-to-become that it's best if becoming stays unrealized, to keep creative sparks alive? Under whose feet is the ground solid enough to say so?

Here is the perdition of philosophy. Musing on the reality of "this," it neglects the reality of "that," which is Anzia, bent over by pain and crouched to the floor. She is passing her hands over the harsh braided rug as if to gather something up. The cloth at the throat of her shirtwaist soaks up tears.

"He'll come back," she said aloud. "He can't renounce life." She was making those gathering movements with her hands, imitating the way Bill Dow would gather up John's poems from his wastebasket the minute he saw them there and take them to the curator of the archives. They won't be lost, she thought, and that was her comfort now.

Suddenly, her hands dove at her cheeks with a sharp, clapping sound. An urgent voice spoke itself clearly in her head. It's not safe to throw the poems away now. The curator and Bill Dow are *both* on vacation!

26 ···≼

End of a Project

The note, written on heavy paper, at the top of which Barnes's initials rose up like jewels in a coronet, was delivered by Barnes's driver. It named an afternoon hour at which Marsh would meet with Anzia. She roused herself from her bed, where she had been mourning John's poems. John will come back, she thought, but the poems will never come again.

Now he'll ask me for the painting, she thought, waiting for Marsh in the parlor. Barnes must have sent him.

His broad, rough strength was always elegantly clothed. Today Marsh's dark, pin-striped suit still seemed in its newness to bear the tiny pricks of the finisher's needle.

She expected to hear him demand, Where's Dr. Barnes's naked woman?

Instead, he lounged against the yellow-papered wall. He regarded her at his leisure for a long moment. When he matter-of-factly said, "I've got her back," she was at first bewildered.

"Who? Who back?"

Something like grim amusement played over a corner of his mouth. "You stirred them up at the precinct, I'll say that. We had to take care of some of those guys. Not to mention the guardians of morals among the school officials. Tickets to the policemen's clambake. New window shades in the classrooms. See what I mean?"

As if there had been no insult. As if he was taking her into his confidence. Any minute she expected to hear him complain, "Why can't Dr. Barnes paint?"

She was wearing her old mended shirtwaist, the one she had worn on the day she first walked into John's office. Her fingers kneaded at the raised scar in the cloth, and she pressed hard on the place, trying to push down on the thumping beneath it.

"Mrs. Dewey"—Marsh took a cigar from his vest pocket, ran a match along the rough varnish at the lip of a table plank, and sucked in a huge yellow flame—"took the professor to the farm, you know. Summer's about over. We don't expect them back. Between you and me"—he leaned his heavy chest forward in a ponderous pause—"this project's about over, you see what I mean?"

She sank onto an ottoman, whose surface was as hard as a stale baked roll, while he took a few luxurious puffs on his cigar, then shrewdly watched her watching him through the smoke.

"Cheer up. You held your own for a while. Under the circumstances, you didn't even do so badly. Your odds were never that good."

She found it hard to breathe. "If you think that, you don't know anything about it. I never should have accepted the painting from Barnes."

"Suppose you didn't, and then suppose one day the professor 'heard, anyway, that a painting disappeared from Merion? Suppose we had the rooms searched and discovered it was in yours?"

"I don't believe you'd do that. I don't believe it of Barnes."

He thrust his big head forward, demanding that she pay attention, feel the terror of torn and intricate selves. "How the hell do you know what we would or wouldn't do? Or what's inside a man like him?"

He returned to his silent, unhurried watching of her.

"Did you think you were going to succeed like me? A nobody, taken up by a great man? Then you couldn't afford to make mistakes. No mistakes, I tell you! Oh, I watched you. I mentally placed my bets. This comes as no surprise to me. Too many mistakes! But I'll tell you one thing. There isn't anyone in this world who's in a better position than I am to appreciate the effort you put in. I might even say, just between us, there's a little ingratitude here." He nodded his head. "The professor failed to show the kind of gratitude Dr. Barnes does."

She pushed herself to her feet. "Do you think we're speaking of master and servant here? He rescued me, I rescued him."

Marsh groaned. "Oh, Christ—is that what you think?"

"John won't give up his new life just when he's discovered it."

"Discovered? Maybe. The way Columbus discovered America, on the way to someplace else."

"I am necessary to him!"

" 'That which is necessary does not offend me,' " Marsh quoted with pride. "Know who said that?"

She covered her ears with her hands. "I don't want to know."

He pulled roughly at her wrists. "Nietzsche! Nietzsche! See— I'm one of the people getting an education too. Add it to your notebook. A present from me."

For some reason Marsh was now furious at her. He began a sneering summing up. "You got what you wanted, didn't you? A little learning, a little shine rubbed up on you to help you make your way in America?"

She was the one stuck now beneath the fire escape looking up. And Marsh was flinging down the flowerpot. "Now forget he was ever in your life!"

It was that quick, sharp pain, coming in the midst of misery, that cleared her head. She suddenly saw what could happen now. If she kept up her courage she could *make* it happen.

27

Poetry Restored

A N Z I A

The office is locked, the corridor deserted except for a porter mopping the floor at the far end, swishing water and disinfectant. He is moving toward me. He hums in rhythm to the motions of his big mop.

I hurry toward him. I pretend I'm breathless and in a rush. I *am* breathless and in a rush, but from terror. I say I'm a member of Professor Dewey's Philadelphia project. The professor, I say, is in a big hurry for some papers he left behind.

The porter doesn't stop mopping. He's got a sixth sense for liars.

"So the professor can go on with his work, I'll need to get into his office right away. I'm sorry to disturb you." I shout a little. I don't want to come too near and print my dirty boot sole on the clean swipes.

He is a Negro with a large, solid body and a long, dignified head. His eyes are half-lidded. He's been listening to his song. He won't say he doesn't believe me. He just goes on mopping without singing.

"The professor forgot some of his papers."

I begin again. My fake signs of breathlessness have become real in my throat and chest, which feel pounded now by giant fists.

"He sent me for them." I am taking agitated steps back and forth in front of him. I think of how it might be if I suddenly slipped in the wet, the way I fell by the riverbank. "The professor was sure you'd have the keys. Thank you." I'm hopping, skipping, back and forth, catching his attention. I thought my ankle was better; now it hurts again, reminding me. "Please open the door for me."

The man lifts the pole of his mop before plunging it into a deep metal pail. For a moment it hangs before me with its long hair like a chopped-off head. His hands are thickened with work, but I can see how the long finger tendons move, how the fingers holding the mop handle have round, padded, tipped-up finger ends, like a musician's. I wonder if he might be a musician, like the men Barnes brought in to sing.

I rattle on blindly, praying the right words will come. "In Philadelphia the professor and the project members heard a group sing some wonderful spirituals. They sang them right," I said, "not like here when white people put on a show and all the tunes get spoiled. The professor wants the notes he made about that."

A thick bunch of keys hangs at his belt. Selecting one and moving with a slow tread—he is humming in rhythm to his walking—he approaches John's office. He holds open for me the heavy door, half wood, half meshed glass, through which I first entered John's life.

I almost feel that John might be there now. Or else he might come in. Suppose he does and finds me kneeling at his garbage? Or suppose it's Marsh? Or Barnes? They always seem to know where I am. I see Barnes as he was in my dream, lifting his head, heavy as a bear's.

I know her kind, Marsh will think. Or Barnes will. Women like that. Grabbers. I can see Marsh in his pin-striped suit, smoking his cigar. Barnes with his fur collar bristling under his jaw. There I'd be, pinned in a crouch over the wastebasket.

"I better stay while you get it," the porter says in a quiet voice, while he glances around the office.

John's desktop is cleared. But the wastebasket is filled to

the rim with the familiar, loosely crumpled yellow papers. It sags heavily to one side. *Let it be there!*

I place my string bag over the mouth of the basket and shake upside down. Yellow paper balls tumble lightly in, then something heavy and solid thuds down. My heart thuds with it. The manuscript of poems is in my net.

The porter blocks the doorway. "How come you taking trash?"

Oh, no, not now! Don't stop me now! I put a tone into my voice I've never used before. A jokey, cheerful, chuckling sound, to cover all my misery.

"You know how absentminded the professor is." I'm smiling hard. "He put the manuscript in the wastebasket and is probably carrying trash around right now in his briefcase."

"Unh-hunh!" He laughs, he shines up his voice for me the way I shine mine up for him. He allows me, with my desperate joke and heavy bag, to pass. He hums a rhythm in counterpoint to the slamming of the door. "Unh"—*thump!*—"hunh!"

In my mind I address Harry Marsh, or maybe it's Albert Barnes. I can learn even from you.

I carry away the shawl-wrapped bundle of poems in my arms like a kidnapped baby. In my old Lower East Side room I throw myself and the poems on the bed and press them to my body. I feel I'm nourishing them again. Later I read and reread, and they nourish me. I know their faults. How can they bother me now? All I see is miracle. They exist.

Night after night, when I return from work, I read them over. Sometimes I shut my eyes and recite them by heart. Other times I caress the lines of text with my eyes.

"Only here matters. These pages."

I must keep the manuscript till the start of the new academic year, when I know the curator and Dow will be back. Reading the poems and reliving the past are not so painful now that I am shaping a plan. I'm not so compelled to reread them every night. I'm rehearsing in my head what I will soon undertake to do. I believe that by the start of the fall term it will be an easy matter for me to pass one day through the familiar hallways. To choose a time according to the lecture schedule I know so well. To elude Dow, whose uneven heartbeat step I can identify with eyes closed. To reenter with the treasure.

But I put it off.

I wait. In the fall, on November 11, the Armistice is declared. First I hear it shouted in the streets, then I read about it in the papers. Congress defeats Wilson's peace proposals and vetoes the entry of the United States into the League of Nations. The newspapers report that Paderewski played Chopin's *Polonnaise* at the signing of the Treaty at Versailles. I know what that means—the failure of the Polish project, the defeat of democracy in Poland. Rumors circulate that Wilson has suffered a nervous breakdown. Yet the country goes on believing he is a whole man. Of how many men, I wonder, does the country go on believing that? And still I can't part with the poems.

One day a photograph of John appears in the *World*. I clip it out and paste it in my journal. He is on the deck of an ocean liner, a converted troopship reconverted. Alice is with him at the rail. A breeze fans them. I restrain myself. I don't, like a fool, try to stroke back the lock of hair that's fallen across his forehead in the photograph. "Common-sense philosopher," says the caption, "sails for Far East for three years." Now I *can't* restore the poems.

Even after I read of John's return to the United States, I keep putting off my task. For three years I put it off, then for another time twice as long. I've grown used to having the poems near me while I polish and publish my stories. My own fortunes rise, and Louise at last comes to live with me. A movie is made of my stories in Hollywood, where they call me the "Sweatshop Cinderella." Another name for me to hate. As if I went overnight from low to high, without struggle.

I wait. I put it off. I am watching. What John did before he does again. Volume after volume appears, filled with analysis of the issues of our lives: immigration, education, labor unions, politics, social action, ethics, science, law. His publications pile up—*Human Nature and Conduct, The Public and Its Problems, Characters and Events*. Then there are the books on experience—*Experience and Nature, Experience and Education, Art as Experience*. There is even a book co-authored with Barnes: *Art and Education*. Nothing for society's good lacks John's corrective counsel. He is honored by testimonial dinners and speeches, bound up for him in presentation leather. Public. Abstract. Dry.

170

I publish a review of one of his books, sounding notes to recall him to himself:

> Can it be that this giant of the intellect—this pioneer
> . . . of philosophy has so suppressed the personal in
> himself that his book is devoid of the intimate, self-
> revealing touches that make writing human? Can it be
> that Professor Dewey, for all his large social vision,
> has so choked the feelings in his own heart that he has
> killed in himself the power to reach the masses of peo-
> ple who think with the heart rather than with the head?

I hear his reply as clearly as if he had written a response and mailed it to me: Please. Anzia. You teach me. Vacations, semesters, academic years have passed—ten of them! Finally I go back to Columbia to find John's wastebasket. I have telephoned to check the time of his lecture. With his wrapped-up poems under my arm, I walk the familiar corridors, elude Dow, and for the last time reenter John's office. I expect to be stricken by the emptiness of it, but I don't have time. The wastebasket catches my attention right away. Thank God, it's nearly full, due to be emptied soon by the watchful Dow. All the players are still at their posts!

I slide my hand among the loosely crumpled papers, making a place. The gesture feels unbelievably intimate. I allow John's manuscript of poems to sink to the bottom of the basket and lift some crumpled papers to the top, plumping them up like a warm blanket. I leave as invisibly as I entered.

Then I wait to hear some word. About John. About the curator. About some venturer into the archives. All the past's an archive. Break the lock, shake the box—which memory falls first?

In book after book I write John's portrait, disguised. Educated, gentlemanly Gentiles who at first shine upon the lives of immigrant women like beacons, but in the end are overcome by difficulties with their feelings. I send him copies and picture him curled over in his chair with my books in his lap, letting them teach him, his broad brow furrowed with thought.

I picture Barnes visiting John (Marsh's name has disappeared from newspaper articles about Barnes; Harry Marsh fades

171

from sight like an etching obliterated by acid). Barnes sees my volumes and sneers at their titles—*Hungry Hearts, Salome of the Tenements, Children of Loneliness, Arrant Beggar, All I Could Never Be.*

Over and over. I can hear Barnes. The same old song.

But I never hear about anybody discovering the poems.

New Salomes come to America every day to fill the old tenements with new language. Their tongues swing like shovels at the hard soil of English, breaking it up all over again some new way. They work at menial jobs. They regard Americans like me with awe. I am already displaced.

One day, a face in the newspaper catches my eye—large, frowning, dark-browed. I read the obituary that goes with it. The man who had so much trouble saying no to himself has driven his car through a stop signal. Crushed to death by oncoming traffic. Albert Barnes.

While I am cutting out the obituary to paste in my journal, I start sobbing so violently that the point of the scissors jabs into my thumb. Why cry now? I have no patience with myself. Drops of blood stipple the paper. I wipe at it with a rag. My page looks like an impressionist sunset. I scratch my journal entry over the smears, and violet haloes form around the ink:

> *Albert Barnes had his locked-up pictures. John Dewey has his thrown-away poems. Let me go into the world with all of myself at once!*

I want to know if the poems were ever found. There's no word. There's no one I can ask.

Sometimes I prop up on my writing table that old photograph from the *World* that's pasted in my journal. John and Alice on the deck of a ship, forever sailing away.

I'd like to walk down to the sea, jump in, and swim over to that boat. I'd swim up—I can't swim but I'd swim there. Why not? Why would that be hard? You learn as you go. I can *feel* myself swimming out to that boat, although I can't swim and am nearly drowning myself. I can flail around and hold up somehow, drag my head from the water to tell him, "The poems are safe! They went into the wastebasket at the right time!"

I can push water away from my chest and call up, a voice

from the sea, to remind him, "Don't split off feelings from thoughts!" I call up to him at the railing, or maybe to Alice, who'll be looking around sharp-eyed while he stares out at some spot on the horizon. All the water in the ocean rushing past my lips can't quench my message:

"Don't worry—there's still me in the world to hold all of your selves together in my mind!"

I hold all of him in my mind. And hold with it a day when John and I went to sea a second time and stood naked under the moon's light. For a dollar and seventy-five cents each, John bought two excursion tickets from Philadelphia to Atlantic City, good for fifteen days, though we could only stay for two. Starting out from Market Street, we boarded the Reading Railroad and traveled to the end of the line, a way station on a wharf, then onto a ferry, then another train that moved across the green summer marshes.

Atlantic City was full of life, even in wartime, and John and I stared at everything. Sea light sparkled on the sand. Pennants waved from boardwalk pavilions that shielded soldiers on furlough with wives or sweethearts. They snatched at happiness in the cool shadows, while they gazed their fill at the sun-gold sea.

We snatched at happiness too. We slept at a hotel called the Revere, on Park Place, smaller than the grand hotels that faced the ocean. Seclusion was just what we wanted. We strolled the boardwalk, ate our dinner, then returned to make love in a room that was flooded with moonbeams and smelled of the sea.

Some of the fine white sand has sifted into our clothing. It falls to the floor as we undress for our first embrace in the seeming dark after the brilliant outdoors. And late at night again, when the suddenness of a poem sends John bolting from bed to desk, more sand is scattered. John blows a few grains from the paper. He laughs and says it's the old way of drying ink.

He is full of delight, blowing sand around. "Richness and plenty," he says, mouth to my breast.

The grains spatter to the floor.

"Like Sheba's pearls falling," says John, saving it up for one of the stanzas I saved.

Afterword

Because this novel grew from traveling imagination's road, I have sometimes knowingly altered facts (though never major ones) in order to make the journey possible. This does not mean there are not also plenty of nonimaginary facts in it as well. To the reader interested in sorting one from the other, I offer here a few strands separated from what has become for me an almost inextricable interweaving.

Portraits of Dewey and Yezierska are extensions based on their own writings and on the writings of those who encountered them. In the case of Yezierska, sometimes the biographical facts are at odds with the re-created self in Anzia's own novels. On occasion one fiction writer (myself) has accepted the other fiction writer's (Anzia's) view, which has made its own forceful imaginative way and taken over the mythology of her life.

Official biographies of Dewey read like a Victorian's model of the Industrious and Virtuous Lad. However, here and there a word casually dropped in an associate's memoir, and especially the publication of the poems themselves, have provided hints of other paths to pursue.

The Philadelphia project was a reality and was written up by Dewey in a real Confidential Report. Scholars have analyzed the project in detail (without of course mentioning what concerns us most here). The real group of researchers involved in the actual Barnes-Dewey project in the summer of 1918 were serious Dewey students, and all went on to responsible careers in philosophy and related fields. I have not attempted to portray them or their achievements here, since they are minor to my story.

Concerning Albert C. Barnes, the collector famous for his art and bad temper, the truth is that he was there in New York and Philadelphia then and is with them here. And though I have invented some nasty lines for him, they seem no worse than ones set down from memory by those who knew him. Because Barnes was such a busy man, I created an assistant for him, Harry Marsh.

What might appear to be the bizarrest of inventions—the snooping habits of the curator of a great university and his secret salvaging of every Dewey scrap—is fact. Upon this overburdened official, I bestowed the co-conspirator, Bill Dow.

The recovery of the poems came about in this way: One day, a decade after the Dewey-Yezierska affair had ended, the Curator of Columbia University's Butler Library, Milton Halsey Thomas, discovered the poems in Dewey's wastebasket. He naturally assumed that Dewey had placed them there and at once secreted them in the Dewey archives. In my view there was ample reason, space, and time for Anzia's redemptive intervention, as depicted in the closing pages of this book. Here the reality of imagination supersedes, for me, Thomas's imagining of a fact.

Yezierska's review of Dewey's published work is recounted verbatim, as are lines from the Scudder Klyce correspondence, though the latter was in reality written a few years after the date at which I have set it. Randolph S. Bourne's essay in Seven Arts is quoted from, as is Dewey's report to President Wilson. Dewey's poems are inventions, written by me, attempting to capture the technique and tonality I found in the originals.

Finally, the Dewey-Yezierska connection itself is as much fact as can be attested to by Yezierska's stories and Dewey's poems and suggests an abundance of themes for the imagination. A Cinderella story? In some ways, yes, we see that she was for a time rescued by him, though soon enough she was *poor and obscure again. A tale of exploitation of a powerless woman by a powerful man? Possibly that is never to be discounted, despite Dewey's essential decency. Yet how speak of exploitation, when imagination is warming the few available facts to a story of mutual completion? ("The two halves of a single egg, they once were split asunder-O/ And all our mortal lives are spent gluing up the blunder-O.")*

If Yezierska is a Cinderella manqué, what is Dewey? We still lack the myth name for a man who is rescued from the ashes by a woman.

As to the country perennially renewed in hope by its newcomers, we are (as the fairy tales say) living there still.

Acknowledgments

For generously reading the manuscript in search of philosophical flaws, I am grateful to Dr. Ruth Dowd, R.S.C.J., Professor of Philosophy at Manhattanville College, and to Dr. Muriel Dance, aficionado of both Dewey and Yezierska. If errors concerning Dewey's work have crept in, they are mine alone.

In addition, Dr. Howard B. Gotlieb, Director of Special Collections, Mugar Library, Boston University, gave wise counsel concerning the Yezierska manuscripts.

My editor, Joyce Engelson, generously shared with me her memories of Anzia Yezierska from the days when Ms. Engelson was a very young writer interviewing the old Yezierska. I have shamelessly appropriated that aspect of Ms. Engelson's persona for my narrator.

Two indispensable volumes have been *The Poems of John Dewey*, edited by Jo Ann Boydston, who is also the scholar-sleuth who traced the Dewey-Yezierska connection through watermarks and typefaces, and *Anzia Yezierska, A Writer's Life*, by her daughter, Louise Levitas Henriksen. Although my manuscript was completed before the publication of the latter, it provided a base against which to check, as well as a thrilling confirmation of much that I had conjectured. I have met these authors through their work, and thank them.

177